THE COPPER TARNISH

Éric Desmarais

www.RiverCitySirenPress.com

Cover art, typesetting, and cover design by Éric Desmarais

Editing by Jen Desmarais, Anne Coderre, and River City Siren Press.

Paperback ISBN: 978-1-964989-18-1

Hardcover ISBN: 978-1-964989-19-8

Ebook ASIN: B0F8KRR6N5

To Adrien,
whose sleepless nights fuelled the weirdness
of this book, and hugs infused it with love.

Author's Note

The following novel is based in the Aetherverse, the shared universe of books by my wife, Jen Desmarais, and I. Because of this, I chose to keep the spelling and the setting Canadian, meaning there are a lot more "U"s and mentions of Canadian things. All temperatures are in celcius.

The setting is extremely rural, in a very tiny town. It's vaguely based on the town I grew up in.

Assume anything that's non-supernatural and weird is due to the setting.

Be warned there is a lot of homophobia, biphobia, xenophobia, talk of sex, gun violence, and goo that takes over people's minds.

CHAPTER 1

Imagine it: high school 2015, or, as I like to call it: Hell. Senior year should have been my chance to rule this school. Unfortunately, in small town Northern Ontario, when you have a bad breakup, everyone knows about it, and when you're falsely accused of killing the asshole, it's even worse.

Instead of ruling with my sense of fashion and my epic culinary skills, I found myself scuttling through the halls trying to avoid all my old friends and my ex. Who hadn't died after all.

"Whoa! Killer Lesbian coming through." Steve towered over most of the other students in the hallways between classes. His light brown hair, square jaw, and freckles made him look like the love interest from a bad sixties' movie. Basically, he was hot; unfortunately, he knew it. He, Chad, and Richard were all leaning in a row against their lockers leering at everyone walking by.

I eyed Richard, my ex, and said, "You need him to fight your battles now?" Richard lived his name, he was the stereotype of a Richie or Rich; jet black hair, tanned skin, skinny but defined, makes me drool just thinking about him. Since our breakup though, his skin had become a sickly beige and his eyes were disturbingly green, like neon lights shining in his face.

It was hard to see into those eyes without getting a chill, and not the good kind. Robotically, he said, "I have no battles to fight, Helen."

"You're totally right, bro. This Lesbo isn't worth the trouble. Let's get the hell out of here." I kept my eyes on Steve's hips as he walked past me. He was a hockey player, and not a good one. His hips told me which direction he was going to move. Which, in this case, was to hip check me.

Swaying away from him, I casually swept my foot toward his. He was already unbalanced from the attempted hip check and tripped. Dance trumps hockey once again.

Face on the ground, he growled like some sort of bear and was about to say something. He was cut off by Mr. Smith, leaning out of his office, yelling, "Miss Benson! My Office Now!" He was the only person where the capitals on each word were audible when he was pissed.

He waited for me to follow, a stern look on his normally blank face. From the doorway, I watched the bulk of a man move around his desk, stepping over several random piles of papers. When he sat in his chair, his sigh mimicked its squeak. I was good and didn't say anything.

"Sit down, Miss Benson."

The chair across from his desk was the only surface that wasn't covered with papers or discarded candy bar wrappers. The office smelled of sweat and chocolate.

"Sir–"

"No," he interrupted. He took a swig from his disposable coffee cup. It had Benson's Diner written across it. "I'm not sure what's wrong with you this year, but you've changed. You used to be chipper, happy, and helpful. You were student body president, head of the cheer club, and now, Mrs. Ferris says you dropped out of dance." Small towns live on gossip. *Does everyone know my every move?*

"Yes." What else was I supposed to say? I couldn't face Ferris Dance Academy after this summer. When your best friends turn on you, it's hard to forgive them. Extra hard when they don't apologize and continue to avoid you.

"Is this about the events of this summer?" He did air quotes around "events." I almost sprained something not rolling my eyes. When I didn't answer, he said, "Everyone knows that you didn't do anything wrong." He should tell that to the people that cross the street to avoid me.

"I just changed my priorities this summer, sir." From the look he gave me, he didn't believe it. I needed to distract him before he continued to pry into what happened this summer. "I'm trying to concentrate on my grades." That should hopefully help.

"Your academics are okay, but you'll need extracurriculars to really stand out on a university application."

"You're right, sir. I'll have to find something." I passed my hand through my shoulder length, naturally bright red hair trying to look innocent.

Furrowing his brow, he peered at me over his glasses and tried to take another swig of his coffee, but it was empty. He glared at the cup like it had insulted his family and put it in the nearly-empty trash can. I wondered if I should mention that the candy wrappers could go in there too. "Alright."

"Sir, I'm going home for lunch. Did you want me to bring you back a fresh cup?" I pointed at the coffee cup.

"Um, yes, please. Two sugars–"

I interrupted him: "Three creams and an inch of hot water on the top."

He nodded, impressed. I'm not sure why he was surprised. I'd been making his coffee for four years. One of the weird perks of working for my family's restaurant and café, I got to learn the weird ways my teachers take their coffee.

Before he remembered that he brought me in for tripping another student and that he wanted more details about what happened this summer, I stood and said, "I should get to my next class."

On my way out, the new girl tried to talk to me. She gave me a little wave and said, "Hi." She'd been trying to get me to chat since school started. It had been a month of me ignoring her, but she still wasn't getting the hint.

"Listen. You seem sweet and all, but stop trying to talk to me."

"Why?" she asked, her large blue eyes getting larger in surprise. She had a soft, breathy but distracted tone to her voice that reminded me of Miss Honey from *Matilda*.

"I'm not a good friend. I'm not someone you want to be around. Don't you pay attention? I'm a social piranha and hanging out with me will kill your chances of fitting in."

Pushing back her long blonde hair, she cocked her head sideways and said, "You mean social pariah. A piranha is a small carnivorous fish, a pariah is someone who is hated. Did you know the word comes from the Indian lower castes? It's a fascinating history."

Her head stayed cocked to the side and she gave me a crooked smirk; this girl was weird. Her clothes would have told me that. She dressed like a beach bum, which would work in L.A. or Vancouver, but in Northern Ontario it just made her stick out. On the other hand, she certainly knew how to dress for her shape. She was plump, but her dress accentuated all her best features. It gave my mind lots to imagine. Her white dress contrasted with her naturally tanned skin. Hormones made life hard.

"Whatever," I said and walked away before my imagination made me blush. She waited a few beats and followed me. My next class was biology, and she was in it. Hard to avoid people when your senior class fits into one classroom.

I took my seat in the back of the class and pulled out my laptop to take notes. "Put your books and computers away. We're having a pop-lab-quiz!" Mrs. Labonté's peppy tone made it sound like she thought it was some sort of a gift.

"Okay, pair off." She checked, saw that I was alone, and her face fell into a deep frown. When she turned and saw the new girl was also alone, she smiled and said, "Seems Bree didn't come today, so Evanna will have to work with Helen." Nodding her satisfaction, she started explaining what we'd have to do for the lab. No books, no notes, just us, an experiment, and a handwritten lab.

"Hi. I'm Evanna Swan, but my friends call me Eve. At least they used to."

"I'm Helen and my friends used to call me Helen." I wasn't sure what to say. She was sad, hot, and weird. I wanted nothing to do with her, but I felt sorry for her. It's not easy fitting into a social hierarchy where everyone else has known each other since they were toddlers.

"That's a terrible nickname. Maybe Elle would be more appropriate?"

"Yeah, they should call her Hell! Cause that's what being her friend was like." Amanda, one of my former dance friends, leaned over from her desk. "Careful new girl. Hell here will try to hit on you and turn you into a lesbian."

Eve looked puzzled, eyebrows furrowed and little upturned nose wrinkled and she said, "That's not how sexuality works. Maybe you should pay more attention to Mrs. Labonté and less to us?" she said in a calm, almost sing-songy way.

I laughed. I couldn't help it. Amanda made a face like she'd sucked a lemon and turned back to her partner.

"Are you a lesbian?" Eve asked in her distracted tone.

"No," I answered too quickly.

In a small rural town like Ansonville, being different was worse than being accused of murder. These people do not tolerate differences, especially when it comes to sexuality. Being a gay man or woman is treated worse than being a leper.

"Oh. Okay." Did she seem disappointed or was my mind playing tricks on me?

After the lab was done and we'd handed in our paper, Eve gave me a hopeful smile and asked, "Do you want to have lunch together?"

"I go home for lunch," I replied and I swear her lower lip became poutier.

"Oh, okay. It's just no one wants to sit with me. I guess I can have lunch in the library again." She turned to leave the class.

"You can come with me if you'd like." The puppy dog eyes she'd given me and the sad pout were too much. Maybe it was hard being the weird new kid.

"That would be exciting. I haven't been to your house yet." She smiled before clarifying, "The diner, I mean." Like a new puppy, she followed me to my car. When she saw it, she said, "Is that a Door Tech electric car?"

"Yeah, my dad bought it for me. He's in Toronto and sends extravagant gifts to make up for never seeing me."

Getting into the driver's seat, I picked up the discarded coffee cups and threw them into the back seat. Maybe I was a little harsh with Mr. Smith, considering the state of my car.

"Sorry for the mess. I don't get many passengers."

"That's okay. Did you know the story behind how coffee was

supposedly discovered?" Eve settled into the passenger seat in the way cats settle into a comfy spot. The movement was sensual and casual at the same time. I wondered if she'd practised being sexy or if it came naturally.

If being gay in a small town wasn't bad enough, being bisexual was worse. Even the gay people avoided you. I'd seen it with one of my gymnastics teachers, and I wasn't going to make any more waves than I already had.

"Is that the one about goats?" I asked, knowing the story.

"Yes, that's the one," she said happily.

"It's printed on the café part of the diner; it was the first thing I could read."

"Oh. That's interesting." Her face was interested and her tone genuine. As I drove through the tiny phobic town, I understood that I'd never heard anyone, besides maybe my mom, say it and mean it.

By the standards of those who live in more populated towns, Ansonville would be considered tiny. When most people think small they think there's only one Walmart and one McDonalds. In Ansonville, there was neither. The closest for both was in Timmins, a one-hour drive. The town had two high schools, one French and one English, with less than five hundred students between them. We had three cops, one pharmacy, and not a supermarket in sight. We did have a Giant Tiger.

There was one hospital and it couldn't even do its own blood work, x-rays, or other tests. Again, that was all in Timmins. If you needed anything fancier than an MRI, you'd have to drive four hours away to North Bay. I did that once when I fell badly and got a concussion.

My walk from home to school would have been a thirty minute walk, but if I drove, it was about five. My house and the school were almost the two furthest points in town.

We drove in silence until we hit the Trans-Canadian Highway and the edge of town. The birch trees and maples around the diner were aflame in reds, yellows, and oranges. The air smelled crisp, and I knew that winter was on the way.

There were a lot of things I hated about Ansonville, but despite its claustrophobic size and its small-minded people, the weather was wonderful. Cold in winter and hot in summer. It was home to majestic trees and lakes, and it was almost never humid.

Getting out of the car, I sighed and said, "This is home."

"It's quaint." Eve sounded impressed despite the connotation of the word *quaint*, and then she asked, "What's its story?"

"It used to be an old town hall. Before Ansonville existed, there was a small town called Montrock. Everyone knows something happened, and in the early twenties someone came up and found the entire town abandoned. No sign where they went or what happened. My great-grandparents came when they opened the copper mines in the fifties, and they thought this was a pretty building. They turned it into a diner. It's been in the family ever since."

"Wow. Those are solid roots." She sounded wistful and a little sad.

I took a deep breath of fall mixed with fry grease and walked toward the entrance. "Where are you from?" If she'd come into town last year, I'd have known her entire life's story before the first day of school. Dance was a hub of town gossip and I made it a point of knowing everyone. I missed feeling important, but I didn't miss the amount of energy it took to stay on top.

"I lived in a small town on Vancouver Island most of my life." Her entire, normally mildly amused, face fell into a frown. "I got in trouble and my mom sent me here to live with my aunt, Samantha Carpenter."

"Oh, I'm sorry to hear that. She's really no-nonsense," I replied.

Miss Carpenter was the editor, head writer, and heart of the Ansonville Weekly News. She was a hard-core workaholic and ridiculously stern.

"It's not that bad. She's almost never at home. I get to do almost anything I want as long as the house is always in order. She even promised to let me write a story for the paper. It's all very exciting."

We went into the diner and I nodded at the truckers that had stopped for lunch. There were a dozen teal coloured booths lining the two walls of windows. Another dozen tables stood between the booths and counter area. The counter had six seats that swiveled. I still loved sitting on them and spinning.

I looked up at the café wall and reread the legend:

The Dancing Goats

Kaldi, a goat herder, had his flock out to eat the best grass and found that when they ate certain bright red berries they would dance around.

He decided to try the fruit and found himself filled with energy. When he showed them to the local monks they told him they were the devil's berries and threw them into the fire.

As they watched the berries melted away and the seeds turned from green to deep brown. The aroma was heavenly and the monk declared the berries had been cleansed by the fire.

They crushed the beans and brewed them like tea, creating the first cup of coffee.

"I like that version," said Eve.

"Kid, how's school?" Fred, a large bearded trucker who stopped for lunch every time he passed through, waved at me from his perch at the counter.

"It sucks. How's shipping?"

He chuckled and shook his head. "Pretty good. I got you a present. It's in the kitchen."

"Fred! You don't need to get us gifts," yelled my mom from the kitchen.

"Bah. If it wasn't for Dancing Goat, I'd be out of a job. I owe you two for saving my business."

As we walked into the kitchen Eve said, "I think I've been to another Dancing Goat?"

"Mom has franchises in Westmeath, Montreal, Nushka, and Giant's Tomb Island. She trained to be a chef–"

"In Paris and Istanbul," my mom interrupted. Her red hair, going white, was tied in a bun, and she had multiple dishes cooking at once. She wore a simple green dress shirt and black skirt with a white apron. She seemed tiny next to the giant stoves as she flitted from one place to another in a controlled chaotic dance. I'd gotten her bright red hair, her love of dance and food, but not her slender frame. I'd gotten my father's taller and curvier frame. I'd also gotten his grey eyes instead of her hazel.

"She fell in love with coffee roasting and brought it back to the diner. She sells coffee beans to half of the province, brews coffee to all the locals. She called it Dancing Goat after the legend."

"That's wonderful." Eve sat on a stool next to the counter. "I'm Eve."

"Nice to meet you Eve. You're Miss Carpenter's niece, right? How does a chicken burger with brie and homemade applesauce sound for lunch?" Mom asked, but I could tell she'd already started two dishes.

"Yes, ma'am, and that sounds wonderful. Thank you," Eve replied.

As I went to sit next to Eve, my Mom stuck her tongue out at me. "Guest or no, pull your weight."

Smiling, I joined her in the cooking and plating. I'd been helping in the kitchen with her for most of my life. It was just like dancing, and it was calming to fall into the familiar steps.

By the time our food was ready, I'd served three customers and started a new batch of coffee. Janice, the server for the lunch rush, looked thankful for the help.

All three of us sat down at the small table in the corner of the kitchen to eat, with Janice taking over for my mom.

"I'm going to miss my ten-minute lunch with you next year." My mom got all misty eyed.

"I'm going to miss this food," I said, pausing and glancing at her for a moment before smiling and adding, "and I'm going to miss you too, Mom."

"Ah, glad it's not just the food."

"Nah, I know all your recipes and Jordan promised to send me anything new."

Jordan was one of the other chefs. My mom and he met on her travels around the world, and he followed her to the diner.

"Do you want to see what Fred brought us?" Mom didn't wait for my answer and jumped off the stool. She went toward two large boxes against the wall near the back exit; both were gift wrapped.

I opened the one with my name on it and found a set of top of the line chef's knives, with a wooden block from Japan. In the other package were another two sets for the restaurant.

"Mom, these are worth more than my first year's tuition. How can he afford it?"

Whispering, she said, "He can't, sweetie. Best not ask any questions. He's a sweetheart, but I'm sure he's into something shady." Mom shrugged and added, "Go say thank you on your way out."

It was already time for us to leave, so I made large coffees for me and Mr. Smith. "Would you like a coffee?" I asked Eve.

Her eyes grew large and she said, "Yes, please. I've only had Timmies since I moved here, and I haven't had fresh roasted since I arrived. There was a little café back home that had the best coffee. It's something I've missed."

Coffees in hand, we headed out. On the way, I stopped at Fred's table and gave him a peck on the cheek. He felt like a grandfather to me. "Thank you. You shouldn't have. I'm going into biochemistry, not cooking," I said.

"With your skill, you should be cooking. It'll give you a way to make some money." His mouth tightened and he glanced toward the parking lot without moving his head. In an even tone, he said, "There's a young man sitting on your car. Do you want me to teach him some manners? I don't care if he's military, no one messes with my little Helen." I wondered how he knew the guy was military.

Looking out the window, I saw there was a man I didn't know in a plain white t-shirt and jeans sitting on my car. He wore aviator sunglasses and could have been a more handsome imitation of James Dean. Anyone who doesn't know who that is needs to listen to more Taylor Swift.

CHAPTER 2

"Helen Benson?" the James Dean impersonator asked. His shirt was a little too tight and it showed his well-formed muscles underneath.

"Whatever you want. Go to hell and get off my car. Final warning."

"I'd like to ask you a few questions." He didn't move but he slid off the aviators and gazed at me with clear amber eyes. I felt a shiver run down my spine, the very good kind this time. It was nice to see someone over the age of twenty that didn't look like shit. Don't get me wrong, there are attractive people in Ansonville, but few of them stay attractive after the hardships of working in the mines. That's not to mention the smoking and drinking. When it comes to health concerns, Ansonville's a good fifty years behind the curve.

"Are you a cop?" I asked, sticking out my hip and trying to glower.

"Um. No. I'm just curious about what happened to you this summer." His eyes widened at the mention of a cop.

"I broke up with my boyfriend and he decided to take a walk in the forest. I was accused of killing him until the asshole walked back into town two months later. That's all that happened." Without waiting for him to reply, I put the coffees on the roof and opened my door. Eve followed suit. Taking the coffees back, I took a big sip from my cup and added, "If you want more information, buy me a drink at the National tonight and I might answer you." I winked at him and got into the car.

I started the car and began to drive away before he got the hint and slid off the car. Somehow he made it look cool. When we were on the road, I burst out into giggles.

"That was very flirty. Is that normal here?" asked Eve, completely serious.

"No, that was all me. I can't believe I winked at him. He was cute though, right?"

"I suppose. He's not my type." Eve didn't say anything else until we were pulling into the school parking lot. When we were parked, she turned to me seriously and asked, "What happened this summer that made everyone hate you so much?"

"I made a mistake and…" I trailed off remembering what had happened and shivered. I hated thinking about it.

"It's okay. You can tell me." Eve put her hand on my thigh. It was warm, as was the expression on her face.

It was too close to pity. How dare she think I needed her pity? I didn't need anyone. I said, "Listen. I worked with you in bio and took pity on you for lunch, but we're not friends. I don't have any friends and I don't want any friends. If you want any, go looking somewhere else."

It was cruel but necessary, she'd thank me someday. To her credit, she didn't burst into tears or make a fuss, she just bowed her head and left. As I watched her go, my hands shook, spilling some coffee.

She had a nice walk, a good swing, and she knew how to work her hips.

I was shaken and angry, not dead.

Mr. Smith's office door was closed so I knocked on it and put the coffee on the little table next to it, right on top of the suggestion box. I hurried down the hall but just when I thought I was safe, I heard his door open and he called out, "Miss Benson."

Turning, I waved at him, tapped my left wrist, and shrugged. This time I *was* safe. He didn't try to follow me. It wasn't that I didn't want to talk to him; it's that I didn't want to talk to him about Richard or anything to do with this summer.

Before the whole breakup and loss of social status, I was both the popular girl and the school resident overachiever. When it came to academics, that hadn't changed. I wanted to be a doctor and the best way to do that was to go to Westmeath University in biochemistry.

The only way to clinch a competitive edge was to do a few advanced classes.

Organic Chemistry was taught by a Westmeath U professor and counted for both high school and university credit. The only downside was that the entire class was taught by teleconference. I got to sit in a tiny room with Dean Francis and stare at a screen for an hour. The room smelled of burning electronics and old garbage; Dean smelled worse.

It was a fifty-fifty chance that Dean would show up and I always preferred the days he didn't. He acted like he was confused but he always had the answers, and I was pretty sure he could pass the final after the first week. He was a jerk but a brilliant one.

"Looking good there, Red," Dean pointed at me with both bony hands forming finger guns. It was his signature move. His signature style was a frilled cowboy shirt and cowboy hat. It was complemented by a horrible rat tail, acne, and yellowed teeth.

"Shut up, Dean!" I buried my nose into my coffee cup. The coffee wouldn't last the class, but the smell would, thankfully.

"Feisty as always. I like!"

I was spared more interaction with the Marlboro Man when the screen turned on and our professor appeared. Doctor Batudev was a leading researcher on evolutionary biomechanics, and he made the class worth dealing with Dean. Every lesson was punctuated with wild metaphors and anecdotes that helped me understand what we were talking about.

At the end of the class, Dean leaned against the doorframe, blocking my way out. "So when are you and I finally going to relieve this sexual tension?"

I'm sure he thought he was being cool. I gagged and said, "Yuck. There's no sexual tension between us."

"Keep playing hard to get. It'll make it so much sweeter when we," he continued in a whisper, "consummate."

Leaning on a door frame isn't a stable position. I kicked his shin and he fell backward hopping on one foot to keep his balance. "Once again, Dean. Yuck!"

He yelled at me as I was leaving: "You'll come around. I'm sure this lesbian thing is just a phase."

I stopped, turned to him, and yelled, "I'm not a lesbian. I just don't like you." Thousands of other comments passed through my head but I decided to leave it at that. Yelling at Dean was like yelling at a badly trained dog. It'll whine and pout but then do the exact same thing again tomorrow.

"I believe he's overcompensating for some sort of emotional or psychological issue." Eve appeared next to me.

"Gah!" I screamed and then added, "Who talks like that?"

"Sorry for startling you." Eve peered up at me and smiled.

I continued toward my last class of the day, English lit. "Why are you following me? You're not in this class."

Biting her lip in an oddly sexual manner, she said, "Why do all the seniors call you a lesbian?"

"Because they're idiots and don't have a clue about human sexuality. Also, none of your business." I shook my head. The new girl was getting me confused and annoyed.

Between Dean and Eve, I was so flustered that when I got to the class I walked into Veronica.

"Um, hi, Helen." Veronica glanced up at me through her long eyelashes and bangs. We were alone in the classroom. I shuffled awkwardly to get out of the doorway and not feel her body heat.

"Hey Roni. How are you doing?"

"I'm okay. I'm really sorry for everything." She seemed genuinely upset. Her long black hair was the same colour as Richard's, her brother, and she had the same fake tan. Just like him, she made my teeth sweat. Good genetics there.

Steve came up behind her from the hall and put his arm around Veronica's shoulders. Glaring at me, he asked her, "Is she hitting on you again?"

"No. Just making awkward conversation," Veronica replied. She gave me a sad sigh and took her seat. She had never seemed that sad or beaten before this summer. I'm not sure if it was her starting to date Steve, her brother disappearing, or what we'd done together, but she wasn't the excited vibrant girl I'd always danced and played music with.

Leaning down, Steve stared me in the eyes and said, "Stay away from her. The last thing she needs is a lesbian like you hitting on her all the time. You know what you are is an abomination against nature. It's a sin!" He grabbed the crucifix around his neck and kissed it before a large smile spread across his face. "It *is* a sin." With that, he turned around chuckling. Nothing good was going to come from that joyful attitude.

At the end of the day, I was almost out of the school when I heard a soft sound that could have been a bird choking. I knew who it was before turning and said, "Hello, Miss Lacroix." The school's youngest teacher and by far hottest teacher seemed to have been waiting for someone.

"Helen, please. Call me Josie. You're a senior now." She smiled and it didn't reach her eyes. She wore a conservative blouse and dress pants in neutral colours and her long straight black hair was in a messy braid. She had been a senior when I was in ninth grade and had done a three year combined teaching and arts degree.

She fiddled with the crucifix around her neck and I tried to cut her off– "I really should be getting home. Lots of homework."

"Helen..." she drifted off and paused. I'd done a fair job of avoiding her and her religious speeches but I knew that her uncomfortable squirming wasn't meant sexually, it was her way of working up to: "Have you considered what we talked about?"

"Yes, Miss." I'm not proud to say I bolted. There's something extra awkward about an attractive person in authority lecturing you about Jesus.

I had had enough of the jerks and bigots that populated Ansonville High School.

Once home, I changed into my waitress uniform and gulped another coffee. In truth, we didn't have a uniform, but I found out that a short emerald skirt and a snug white dress shirt ensured I got plenty of tips. I rinsed the cup and headed downstairs for the dinner shift.

The best part about working at the diner was the clients. They were travellers, truckers, and out of town contractors, but most importantly they weren't locals. The Trans-Canadian Highway provided plenty of business for Ansonville South. The small number of businesses and houses on the highway thrived even when the price of copper fluctuated.

When I came into the kitchen with an order from a family of six, my mom asked, "So who was that guy on your car?"

"No idea. Probably a reporter or something. I flirted with him and told him he could buy me a drink at the National tonight."

"Are you still going to that? I mean, considering—"

"Yes. I have a crown to defend," I said a little too emphatically, cutting her off.

Lifting her left hand, and the spatula in it, mom said, "Good luck, call if you need anything, and be safe."

After my shift, I changed into my outfit, a variation on Wonder Woman's new costume. The pants were comfortable, the heeled leather boots were hot, and the corset made me feel powerful. It was both practical and showed enough cleavage to be gasp worthy. In other words, perfect. It was hovering around zero outside and I wasn't willing to freeze, so I paired it with my zip up Wonder Woman costume hoodie. Richard had bought it for me last Christmas. I almost threw it out when we broke up, but decided that it was just too awesome.

With a new coffee and my toolkit, a set of knives and carving implements rolled into an apron with pockets, I walked down the street to the National Bar and Grill. It had been a tavern before they realized they could make more money selling drinks to minors if the minors were allowed into it. They served greasy food and cheap alcohol. Although they weren't technically supposed to serve anyone under nineteen, the drinking age in Ontario, everyone knew they did.

There were a lot of activities I gave up after this summer, but there were some I just couldn't. That meant making pies for the fall fair in September and cookies for the future Christmas fairs, but my pride was the National's pumpkin carving competition.

I loved everything about fall, but especially Halloween; everything about it was exciting. The fake danger, the sexy outfits, and the candy. It was the one time a year that people allowed themselves to be silly.

The National held an annual pumpkin carving contest. The winner got a gift card and a picture of their pumpkin on the wall of fame. My pumpkins had been on that wall since I was thirteen.

They made quite the night of it; there was also a costume contest and a dance. They were always held the Friday the weekend before Halloween. Bob didn't want to conflict with other parties. This year that meant it was a week before the actual day. This was my last year to win the carving contest, and I wasn't going to waste it just because the entire town hated me. Sometimes I couldn't wait to leave this place but others, I knew I'd miss things like this contest.

When I arrived at the National the day of the contest, the first person I saw was Bob, the owner. His gut fought valiantly against the Thor costume he was wearing. He came up to me and said, "Helen, your pumpkins are awesome, but are you sure you want to do this? It is a crowd vote." That wasn't a great start to the night.

"Bob, I'm doing this. If I lose because they're holding a grudge over something I didn't do, then they're morons, and I tried. Or are you asking me not to participate?"

"Naw. I couldn't do that to you and your mom. You've helped me out too much. Just wanted you to know it'll be extra hard this year." When his wife died, mom had taken over the bar and hired an extra chef at the diner while he grieved.

"Thanks. I'll just have to do something amazing," I smirked and Bob gave me a glare. I quickly said, "No pyrotechnics this year, I promise." He grunted and went back to the bar.

I was fashionably late, since I had to work beforehand, and the four other competitors had already picked their pumpkins. It left me with the ugliest, most gnarled pumpkin in the bunch. I didn't care; as long as it wasn't rotten, I could do something with it.

There was little competition. One of my competitors actually made a smiley face pumpkin. The only real challenger was Allison, the resident hippy and artist. Normally she only worked on wood but always did elaborate pumpkins for the local businesses. She was better than I was and the only reason I always won was her pumpkins were too high concept. She did symbolic vistas, or one year she did a nature landscape. She mostly did it for fun and always gave me carving tips. I'd always thought of her as a kindly grandmother type.

She was the only competitor that even acknowledged I was there. She nodded and told me, "Good luck."

I normally won because I knew a crowd in a bar wanted something cool, sexy, or disgusting. I had decided the best choice this year was to make something weird: a two-faced pumpkin. On the gnarled side, I made a gothic gargoyle, like the ones I'd seen on the Parliament buildings when we'd visited two summers ago. On the other was the current Prime Minister.

I got a lot of heckling as I worked but I ignored them. After two hours we were told to put down our tools. The pumpkins were put on the bar with a little ballot box and people voted.

The pumpkin Allison had carved was gorgeous and disturbing. It showed three miners in a cave. She'd used a green LED light inside which made the whole thing glow an odd colour and melted some metallic wax that looked like oxidized copper onto the miners' faces.

"Why are those miners green?" Eve had sneaked up behind me and startled me again.

Before I could say anything, Allison replied, "It's my interpretation of the 'Copper Tarnish' folk story, dear." She patted Eve on the shoulder and headed to the bar for a drink.

"What's that?" Eve asked me.

"I don't know," I answered truthfully.

"Before you get upset, I bought you a drink as a peace offering." Eve handed me a Drunken Goat, a cup of my mom's coffee that he brewed and poured with a liberal amount of spiced rum. It was perfect for keeping me awake and warming my insides.

"Why?" I sipped the hot cup of joy.

"I was too pushy in asking questions, and I upset you. I sometimes get too nosy. I'm sorry."

"You're forgiven, but it's still a mistake for you to try to be my friend. You'll never fit in with me holding you down."

A smile spread across her face, it was both mischievous and stunning, the perfect combination to make my heart start racing. "Being held down by you doesn't sound too bad, and besides, it's my mistake to make. Maybe you're the only person here I want to fit in with." Her gaze flickered behind me and she continued, "Your mysterious stranger is sitting at a table with two drinks."

"Oh? I didn't think he'd show up."

"Do you need me to be there with you?"

"No, I can handle him. Under that hot, muscled exterior is a mushy interior. Plus, I'm in a crowded bar." I finished my drink and headed to the washroom to get the last of the pumpkin guts off my carving kit, hands, and face. I took my hair out of its ponytail and let it fall loose.

Outside the washroom, I swayed up to the table, doing my best walk and sat across from him. He glanced up from his phone distractedly and said, "I got you a drink."

Laughing, I said, "That's ginger ale."

"You're only eighteen. I really need to know what happened this summer."

"Who are you?"

"That's not important. What happened before Richard Gates disappeared?"

"I'll answer your questions if you answer mine." I took another sip of my coffee and crossed my arms.

Checking around like he was expecting trouble, he said, "No, I—" he paused a little then stared at me intently while saying, "You wouldn't believe me if I told you." Giving him the bitchiest face I could, I shook my head and started to get up.

"Please. It's really important that you tell me what happened," he reiterated.

"You're either the crummiest cop I've ever met or the worst reporter. Richard broke up with me because he caught me making out with someone else. He ran into the woods and I didn't see him for two months. That's it." If I told him the whole truth he wouldn't believe me. I played with my hair, trying to not get angry at him for bringing up the horrible memories.

"Hm. Has he been acting weird?" His voice was disinterested but his eyes were intense.

Getting up, I said, "Nope. That's all you get. Buy me a real drink, give me some actual information, or this conversation is over."

"I can't." I started leaving and he added, "I'm Harold."

"Nice to meet you, Harold. Let's do this again sometime." I drained my ginger ale, picked up my carving toolkit, and left.

I saw Eve near the bar and considered going to chat with her some more when a familiar voice let out a soft moan. Veronica's voice was smooth and sultry as she started to sing. Her band was called the V2s, which was four girls from dance who formed an acapella group. They used pre-recorded instruments and did a lot of moaning and gyrating on stage. It had been five of us with me playing the guitar and violin, but like dance, I wasn't welcome anymore. I missed playing music with someone.

No way I was sticking around for that. I headed for the exit. It was already getting close to midnight and Bob wasn't going to announce the winner until closing at 2am. Normally I'd stay and dance, but I didn't want to dance to the V2s.

The air was cold and after the heat of the bar it was refreshing. I held my breath as I passed Dean and the other smokestacks and headed home. It was only a fifteen-minute walk.

It didn't take long for me to start warming up. I was used to practising my routines outside in the cold; it made doing them in the heat a lot easier. I'm tall and there was a point where our little apartment over the diner wasn't big enough for me to dance without breaking anything.

Thinking about dance made me sad and angry all over again. I was pulled out of my self-loathing midway home by the complete quiet. There were no cars passing by and it was as if all of nature was holding its breath.

Instead of stopping and waiting, I walked faster, and then the silence was broken by the most horrifying howl I'd ever heard. It was the stuff of nightmares. I broke into a full run and by the time I slowed down, I could hear footsteps behind me. They were faint and often drowned out by the new renewed traffic on the highway. I took out my phone and used it as a mirror but I couldn't see anything behind me. *Maybe I'm being paranoid,* I thought.

The diner closed at midnight, and it could have been abandoned with all the signs turned off. I sped up again as I got closer and turned the corner of the building to the back where the entrance to the second-floor apartment was and screamed.

Standing in a pool of greenish light from the lamppost in the middle of the back parking lot, was Richard. Moving impossibly fast, he grabbed my arms, and with a grimace on his face, he asked, "Why were you not affected?"

CHAPTER 3

" You should be ONE! Why are you not ONE?" Richard was yelling, but it sounded like an imitation of emotion.

As I stood frozen in surprise, I stared into his murky green eyes. The memories from that horrible night came back to me, making me feel sick to my stomach. There were two things I could do; I could give in to the sickness and puke all over him, or I could try to escape.

I kicked his right shin. It had worked on Dean, but it didn't work on Richard. He didn't flinch. I smashed my forehead against his as hard as I could, and it didn't even move his head. It only made my already horrible headache worse. Still holding my arms, he pushed me against the wall and hissed at me. It was a weird guttural hiss that made me feel like he'd poured dirt all over me.

"You must be ONE!"

Fighting him with everything I had, I couldn't escape. He was much stronger than he should have been. Years of dance and cheerleading made me strong. I should have been able to at least hurt him.

Leaning in toward me, his hot breath smelled of copper, like pennies or old blood. I kicked him between the legs, and he still didn't react.

Not sure what to do, I spit at him. Where all the hitting and kicking had done nothing, spitting on him had caused him to scream in a high-pitched voice. I saw part of his face bubbling where my saliva had landed. He jumped back and ran away from me, screaming.

I collapsed into a sitting position, shaking from fear. I must have blacked out because the next thing I remember was my mother sitting next to me on the ground, holding my hand, and Sergeant

Bannerman standing in front of me. He was a walking stereotype: a white man of average height with brown hair, Mustache, and a uniform that was a little too tight around the middle.

"Are you feeling up to talking about what happened?" asked the sergeant. His tone was concerned but I saw disgust in his eyes. I wondered how long he'd been there.

"I—" Would they believe me? I decided to tell the truth. My head hurt so much. I was never going to do that again. "I was almost home and Richard surprised me, he grabbed both of my arms." I reached up and rubbed my arms and yelped in pain. I unzipped my hoodie and both my mother and the sergeant gasped at the perfect handprint marks. "He kept saying something about not being one, and then he tried to kiss me." The marks burned and felt cold at the same time like frostburn, the cold, almost sunburn feeling of walking against frigid wind for too long.

The sergeant nodded and said, "Has he talked to you about getting back together?"

"No."

He wrote something in his notepad and asked, "This is quite the revealing costume."

"God help me, Walt, if you say she had it coming I'll slap you so hard, you'll sleep through the lawsuit."

Lifting his hands, he said, "I'm just asking questions, Cheryl."

"Start asking good ones." Mom was pissed.

"What happened after he tried to kiss you?"

"I spit in his face and kicked him in the," I gestured at the sergeant's genital area, "testicles."

Closing his little notebook, he asked, "This sounds like assault to me. Will you be pressing charges?"

"Yes," my mom said at the same time I said, "No."

"Sweetie, you need to press charges."

"I just want to forget it happened. I don't want to deal with more courtrooms or media. Please, Mom."

The sergeant was grim and said, "I'll pick him up and give him a stern talking to. You won't have trouble with him again."

My mom fussed over me and put aloe on my arms before bed. All I wanted was to sleep, and I hoped it was dreamless.

Since that night this summer, I seemed to relive it or weird variations of it every night. I tried not to sleep unless I had to; it's why I drink so much coffee. That night, the nightmares were worse than they'd been since the first week. I woke up in a cold sweat around seven the next morning. Before this summer, I would have gone back to sleep and slept until noon on a Saturday. Instead, I got up and took a shower. The heat made me feel nearly human.

I dressed in a pair of comfortable yoga pants and a Fall Out Boy concert t-shirt. Mom kept the house warm, so even in fall it was a bad idea to wear a sweater indoors.

Another side effect from this summer was massive headaches. I thought it was some sort of weird PTSD, but they always went away with coffee. Maybe it was withdrawal, but minutes after I had a sip, I felt better.

As I sipped coffee in our tiny kitchen, my mother said, "Trauma hangover or regular hangover?" She was teasing me but I could see the concern in the furrow of her brow.

"I had one Drunken Goat and a ginger ale, that's it."

"Okay. Are you up for some company?" She gave me an awkward smile.

"No, but that smile tells me I don't have a choice."

"Father Michael is here and would like to talk with you." My mom's smile told me I was to be on my best behaviour. Father Michael was the Anglican minister, and he had officiated my mother and father's wedding. He'd also counselled my mom after dad ran away with Nicole, the tiny blond trucker. As far as religious people, he was a nice old man. He was tall with white hair and a naturally ruddy complexion.

Peeking my head into the living room, I asked, "Father, have you had breakfast yet?" The last thing I wanted was to be lectured, but I had to be polite for my mom.

"Hello, Helen. No, I haven't, but I'd like to speak to you in private if that's okay." His calm voice was deep and reassuring. It also always put me to sleep.

My mom smiled at me and nodded in approval before saying, "I'll go down and get you whatever you'd like, and the two of you can chat." When he was going to protest, she said, "Father, I own and live above a diner, and that has its privileges." She could have made them in our tiny kitchen but with breakfast already started in the diner it was easier and gave us some privacy. Mom had renovated the whole upstairs when I was a kid, but she didn't want a large kitchen because she said she'd rather put the money into the diner and cook there.

"I'd love some of your famous apple cinnamon pancakes, dear. If it's not too much trouble."

"Fall pancakes and the *new* usual for you?" Mom asked me. She emphasised the *new* since I used to be obsessive about what and how much I ate. Being a competitive dancer meant you always had to eat enough to keep up your energy, but not over do it and get slow. It was about balance more than weight. I would have had more eggs and fruits along with a few pancakes.

Since I gave up on all my old passions, I've found my overwhelming love of potatoes and breakfast meat. My new usual was what most places called a lumberjack's dinner, but for theme's sake we called the miner's last meal. Four kinds of meat, three eggs, two pancakes, fruit, beans, and glorious breakfast potatoes. I had been worried about gaining weight when I dropped dance, but I still ate less than most and found other ways to stay active. I was blessed with my mother's metabolism and my father's inability to stand still. Although the doctors called it ADHD of a mixed type.

The living room, dining room, and kitchen were open concept with neutral coloured walls. There was an island that dominated the kitchen, the dining room was more of just wherever the dining table was and the living room had a large comfy couch, an oversized armchair, and a loveseat.

Sitting on the armchair across from Father Michael, who chose the loveseat, I waited for him to start. His face contorted and he seemed to be having a hard time deciding how to broach whatever topic he was trying to say. Finally, he sighed and said, "I've been approached by members of the community that are worried about you."

"Okay?"

"I won't have the sex talk with you. I'm sure your mother and school have covered that, but it's important that you remember that sex is a highly personal and sometimes even holy experience. It should not be entered into without love."

Fighting the urge to burst into laughter, I said, "Okay." I wasn't sure what else to say to the octogenarian minister trying to give me a spiritual sex talk. "Wait. Are you saying that people are going around saying I have lots of sex?" If I was, it was news to me. As far as I knew, I'd never passed second base with anyone but myself. That was embarrassing but pretty much par for course since this summer.

"There are those who are concerned."

"So the entire town thinks I'm what? Some sort of murder slut?" It wasn't fair of me but I was angry.

His eyes opened wide and he said, "I'm not saying any of that, but if you'd like to talk about the difference between making love and the sin of lust, I'm available for you."

Taking a deep breath, I said, "Thank you, Father. I'm not having *any* sex, let alone a lot of sex. If I ever need to have that conversation, you'll be my first choice."

We sat in awkward silence until my mom came back and then I sat in awkward silence as they made small-talk over breakfast at the dining room table. When he'd finally gone, my mom started to laugh and asked, "Was that 'the sex is a sacred thing and you shouldn't blaspheme by doing it without love' speech?"

Between her giggles, I managed to answer, "Yes. How did you know?"

"When I was your age, we used to prank the kids we didn't like by telling him they were sexually active."

"Looks like someone has brought the practice back." My mom's laughter was contagious.

When we finished giggling, I helped her put the dishes away and she asked, "What are your plans today?"

"There's open training today. I think I'll join a class and let off some steam."

"Okay, have fun and be safe."

She was trying really hard to act naturally, but I could see how worried she was. "I'm okay, and I'll be safer in Timmins than here," I replied, only half joking.

I went down the stairs to the entrance. When I opened the door, Eve was standing there with her fist in the air as if to knock. "Oh. Hello." She looked confused but happy.

"Hi. Can I help you?"

"My aunt sent me over with a pie and a tape recorder," Eve said as if it was a normal thing to do. She even held up the pie as proof. "She'd like to know what happened last night."

"So would I and no comment."

From up the stairs I heard my mom ask, "Did I hear pie?"

The box was from CiCi's bakery which was the best, and only, place to buy dessert. "It's a Caramel Apple Pie from CiCi's." I yelled up.

"Invite the pie up. I mean your friend." Mom had a shameless sweet tooth. She didn't make the desserts for the diner; she said it was too tempting to taste them. She had an agreement with CiCi to supply the desserts and mom stayed as far away from them as possible. Unless someone wanted something from her, then they bribed her with pie.

"Would you like to come up for a slice of pie?" I asked. There was always room for pie and I had lots of time.

"That would be nice. Thank you." Eve curtsied. She actually curtsied.

In the kitchen, mom was standing with a pie knife and three plates already on the counter. I was still full from breakfast but agreed to a small slice. It was really good pie. We set up at the island which had three chairs.

"Can I ask you some questions about last night?" asked Eve, as if she was asking for the time or about the weather.

"For you or the newspaper?" I asked. I liked talking to Eve, but I didn't want anything in the paper that would make my life harder.

"My aunt will want something for the paper. But if you don't want to, that's okay."

"I'd rather not." Richard was being a jerk but I didn't want him to face the same media circus I had. Even though Eve's aunt and the local paper hadn't been judgmental, I didn't want to risk him getting hurt.

"Then personally... are you okay?" Eve's deep blue eyes creased at the sides like a puppy who was a little too worried. Her face was warm and her eyes were concerned. I liked how genuine she was.

"Not really, but I should be. I was actually heading out for a visit to Timmins." I spent so much time hiding or ignoring my feelings that I didn't always know what they were.

"Oh. I'll get out of your hair." She looked even more sad and like a puppy. I just wanted to hug her.

My mom's face fell. She obviously liked Eve, and would prefer I didn't go out alone. Mom said, "Why don't you go with her? I'm sure she could use the company. It's over an hour's drive." I'm sure she meant the best but my heart sank. I wanted to take a break from Ansonville, not bring some of it with me. Especially not a confusing part. I was still not sure if I should be attracted or scared about how Eve seemed to be pseudo-stalking me.

"I would like that very much." Eve turned to me and added, "Please?" Her eyes kept the puppy dog aspect, but this time it was coupled with a pouty lower lip.

"Fine. Do you have workout clothes?"

"No. Not really. I only had one suitcase when I moved."

"You can use some of mine, if you roll up the pants and sleeves. That outfit isn't going to work for a Karate class." I looked her up and down, in the long deep blue dress she was wearing, she'd hurt herself. She was much shorter and a little curvier than me, but I guessed she'd fit in some of mine.

I went to my bedroom off the living room and behind the couch and grabbed some extra clothes and added them to my gym bag. Now I had two tops, and two yoga pants. My room was a whirlwind of clothes, books, and stuff. The only area that was completely organized was my music corner with my guitar and violin. I was already wearing a sports bra and Eve would have to use whatever she had on her. No way she'd fit in mine. With the bag in hand I said bye to my mom and we headed out.

In the car she asked, "I thought you did dance, not Karate."

"I gave up dancing because everyone looked at me like I was about to explode and kill them, the other seniors refused to let me change with them, and it just didn't seem as important after everything that had happened."

"You mean where they accused you of killing Richard?"

"Yeah. The thing with activities that you've done and enjoyed since you're young is, they become part of your identity. Losing dance was like losing a part of who I was." I forced myself not to cry, it makes driving extra hard.

Eve made a *hmm* noise of sympathy and asked, "What about other studios?"

"All the other studios had heard I was a bad seed and there were rumours I'd sexually assaulted another student. All made up by my ex and his sister. No other studio would let me join. I was researching community centre dance classes in Timmins when I saw a group of girls our age practising Karate. I watched for a long time before asking if I could join. Practices are unfortunately twice a week, and I couldn't get out on top of my shifts. They do have open sessions twice a month that anyone could join."

"That's where we're going? I've never done Karate, only some Tai-chi." Eve sounded excited.

"It's fun, but I'm not really good at combat. Learning the martial routines, they call them Katas, is a lot like dancing and extremely relaxing."

"Thank you for taking me with you. I'm sorry that I sort of intruded on your day."

"That's okay. It's nice to talk with someone other than my mom or the diner clients." It was true. She was extremely easy to talk to and I found myself comfortable with her.

"What music do you like?" she asked.

"To listen to or play?" I asked.

"You danced and played music. Wow." Her tone was impressed, and I could see her biting her lower lip, making me very distracted.

I gave a soft chuckle. "My mom taught me some basic piano, and I took violin classes when I was young. That's how I first got into dance; I did fiddle and step competitions all across Ontario."

"What's the difference between a violin and a fiddle?"

I smiled and replied, "Just the way you play it, mostly major notes for violin and minor ones for fiddle. I'm more comfortable with fiddling, but I can play some classical too. It's relaxing, but my mom gets pissed when I play at night. That's why I have the electric guitar." Okay, I was showing off, but I had a crush and multiple talents.

"Wow. I only play the flute. It's a special kind that I learned to carve from the Musqueam indigenous elders back home."

"That's seriously cool. We should jam sometime."

She blushed but nodded.

I had so many questions about the flute, but she changed the subject before I had the chance.

We talked about music, books, movies, classes, and all kinds of things on the way. It was nice to have a friend again.

The class was structured into three parts, Kata practice, striking and blocking practice, and then open sparring. I normally didn't participate in sparring but I wanted to show off a little. I found myself wanting to impress Eve.

My first sparring partner was a young girl that looked like she'd break under a brisk wind. I would have expected it to be an easy fight if it wasn't for her blackbelt. I was tossed around like a rag doll, but afterward, she showed me how to block the throws.

I challenged Eve and she bit her bottom lip before closing her eyes and shaking her head. "It wouldn't be fair. I just started." I asked because I didn't want her to feel left out. It was probably for the best, my mind was running through too many bad fanfic scenarios.

The drop-in class was exactly what I needed, a heavy workout that left my muscles sore and me needing a shower. I was thankful we were far enough away from home that there was no way I'd run into an ex dance friend. The showers were individual stalls with a shower and room to change. The heat felt nice but the ache in my muscles felt better.

After getting cleaned up, I asked, "Was there anything you wanted to do?"

"Lunch would be nice."

I knew just the place. There was a small family bakery that made the best smoked meat on rye sandwiches. They also served some of my mom's coffee. We picked some up and drove to Gillies Lake beach. It was a small lake inside the city limits and had picnic tables. It was really clean, and because of the cool weather, we were pretty much alone. I lent Eve the blanket that I kept in my car, since she didn't have a coat.

As we sat down with our sandwiches, chips, and drinks she cocked her eyebrow at me and asked, "Is this where you take all your dates?"

"Is this a date?" I had taken Veronica here once, but it hadn't started as a date.

"That's what I'm trying to figure out." Eve said it matter of factly but her eyes were nervous.

"I don't know. I did bring someone here once, but it ended badly." My voice cracked and I couldn't keep the sadness from it.

"Oh?" The concerned scrunch of her nose was adorable.

Why was I so eager to tell her anything she asked? Maybe it was her intense eyes or maybe I was just attracted to her. "My boyfriend caught us. Making out." I was still embarrassed at my weakness.

"Ouch. Let's call this a friendly outing. That way we can avoid uncomfortable associations."

Did that mean she wanted it to be a date? I wasn't sure but I was certainly enjoying my time with her. When lunch was done, I suggested we go shopping.

Ansonville had a Giant Tiger and a handful of boutique stores, but it didn't have any of the big brand name stores that Timmins Square had.

"Let's get you some less west coast hippy outfits," I suggested. It was a little harsh but she needed something for winter. "Your clothes are cute but you'll freeze in winter if you don't have some sweaters."

"But winter's not for another couple of months," Eve said, obviously perplexed.

I couldn't help but laugh a little, "In Northern Ontario, the first permanent snow normally arrives early November. Winter's not a few months away, it's a few weeks."

"That's not fun. I really do need clothes, I guess."

We went to a bunch of stores and I came out with three comfy cowlneck sweaters and a bunch of fuzzy pyjama pants. Eve, on the other hand, was extremely excited to buy sweater dresses and leggings.

"They were too warm back..." she trailed off and paused, "in Vancouver."

On the way home, we chatted about clothes and sang with the radio. When we were fifteen minutes away from the diner, we saw a police cruiser on the side of the road with its emergency lights flashing. We slowed down and Richard came out from behind the car and tried to flag us down.

"Does he look strange?" Eve asked, and I saw that he had some sort of green stuff all over his shirt.

"I don't want to stop," I said, feeling like a giant wimp.

"Neither do I," echoed Eve.

As we passed by, I saw Sergeant Bannerman laying on the ground behind the car. He wasn't moving.

Chapter 4

"We have to make sure he's okay," I said, my voice cracking. I stopped the car and reached for the door, but Eve put a hand on my arm.

"Shouldn't we call the police?"

"He is the police. There's only three of them. This isn't a big city."

"I don't like this." She was worried.

"Me neither. Stay in the car and call 911. I'll make sure he's okay." Not giving her a chance to argue, I jumped out of the car and ran across the street to Sergeant Bannerman.

Ignoring that Richard was coming around, I checked to see if the sergeant had a pulse. He didn't. I checked his mouth to make sure nothing was blocking his airway and started CPR. Richard's shadow draped over us in the afternoon light.

After about five minutes, my arms were starting to ache and I was about to give up hope when the sergeant took a deep breath. That's when I felt Richard grab me by the shoulders, and with way too much strength, he threw me into the road.

I actually bounced and was glad I was wearing a coat or I would have scratched up my entire arm. I lay there with the breath knocked out of me and listened. The car door opened, and I heard Eve yelling, "Get the hell away from her, asshole!" Then, she gasped.

"Now missy, just get back into the car," drawled the sergeant, his words punctuated by a clicking noise.

I heard Eve whimper and get back into the car. Then I heard the sergeant coming toward me. I lifted my spinning head and saw he was holding his gun casually at his side. Richard grabbed my head and smashed it against the road, the pain was blinding, before placing his hand on my chin and the other on my forehead, forcing my mouth open. Everything felt like a dream at this point dulled by the pain in my head.

Sauntering up, the sergeant knelt next to me. I could have sworn his eyes had become a dull green. He opened his mouth and started making gagging noises. I struggled, trying to push the sergeant or Richard away, but they wouldn't move. I started to panic, and scratched at Richard's face; it did nothing. His skin felt like hardened leather. I finally tried to take his hands off me, but they were like steel grips.

I saw the odd green liquid coming out of the sergeant's mouth and did the only thing I could: I covered my mouth with my hands and closed my eyes. The liquid was thick and hot like warm pudding; even with my eyes closed, it stung. They didn't seem to care too much if any of it got in my mouth.

Just as I thought I would have to move my hand to breathe, I heard the ambulance's siren. Richard let go of me, and I made the mistake of opening my eyes. The green goo dripped into my eyes and started to burn. I closed them again, but it didn't help.

In unison, Richard and the sergeant said, "Now you will be ONE!"

The paramedics asked the sergeant how he was feeling, and he replied, "I'm perfectly healthy. The girl is the one who is hurt."

Even when I opened my eyes, I couldn't see anything. I heard the crunching of shoes on asphalt and a man's voice asking, "Helen, it's Yannick. Where does it hurt?" I tried really hard not to panic but the numbness was fading, and all I could feel was pain and fear.

I lifted my hands to feel my face and it was completely dry. I blinked a few times and still couldn't see. "My eyes. I can't see, and they burn." I tried to sound calm but my voice was shrill and scared.

"Did you get anything in them?"

"Yes, but I don't know what it was." I made the decision not to tell him about the sergeant coming back from the dead, threatening my friend, and projectile vomiting on my face while my ex held me down. Just thinking about it made me wonder if I was hallucinating.

"I'm going to wash your eyes out with some water, they seem to have turned green from whatever is in them." If they were green then maybe I wasn't imagining anything. He rinsed my eyes out, and it felt a little better. He asked a whole lot of questions about what had gotten into them.

"Eve! Is she okay?"

"She's fine. The sergeant has just finished talking with her," he said as he poured cool water onto my eyeball. It felt weird, but it helped with the burning sensation. I yelped in surprise and worry when he mentioned the sergeant and he added, "Sorry. This is necessary. I need to get this stuff out." He misinterpreted my worry for Eve as pain.

As the water washed away whatever vomit was in my eyes, I started to see blurry shapes. It was easy to tell which shape was Yannick. He was tall, thin, and wearing lots of blue.

The other shape, I hoped I recognized. "Eve? Is that you? What happened?"

She bent over and put a hand on my arm. Whispering, she said, "I'm fine. I'll tell you later. What's wrong with her eyes?"

"You can tell her, you have my permission," I said to avoid any issues with personal information.

"She seems to have gotten some sort of chemical into them. We'll know better when we get her to the hospital."

"Can I go with you?" she asked.

"Family only, sorry."

"Eve, can you please drive my car back and tell my mom that I'm in the hospital?"

"Sure. What hospital are you taking her to?"

I couldn't see it, but I imagined Yannick's confused face. We were almost in Ansonville and there was only one hospital in town. The next closest hospital was forty minutes away.

"Iroquois General Hospital," he replied professionally. It was a combination of hospital and doctor's offices. In the emergency room, I was seen right away. That was odd; there were other people ahead of me, but I guess the ambulance had called ahead and I was worse off than I'd thought.

The doctor said a bunch of medical words to the nurses as I was brought to a room. The room was blurry and beige. It made no sense to me but felt like I was on a hospital show. When we were in the room, the doctor checked my head and then my eyes. He also took my blood pressure and listened to my breathing. He was blurry, but I knew he had a mustache and little hair on his head. His calm tone with a hint of an Irish accent was soothing to me. My head was pounding. When he was done he asked, "Helen, do you know where you are?"

"I'm in an examination room at the Iroquois General. Not sure which one."

"And do you know today's date?"

"Yes. It's October twenty-fourth."

The doctor took a deep breath and said, "You've gotten something in your eye. It seems to be acidic. I'm going to clean it out, but I have to get a sample to know what we're dealing with. It might hurt."

"My eyes are burning already, so go ahead."

I felt the nurse's cold hands holding my head and had to take a few deep breaths not to panic. The sample taking didn't hurt. I didn't feel it, and I didn't feel him cleaning my eyes out either. When he was done, he asked, "Does that feel any better?"

It felt a little better and I could make out a little more than I had before.

The Doctor told me he'd come back when the lab had processed my tests. Besides the eye swab, he also took blood tests.

"We've called your mom. She'll be here soon. Just rest," the nurse said as she put a heart monitor on me. I was sure I wouldn't be able to sleep with the beeping. Everything swirled through my head, and I felt like I should be terrified but I was just tired.

I fell into a dreamless sleep until my mom and Eve arrived.

"How are you feeling, sweetie?" My mom sounded like she'd been crying.

"Like crap and I'm terrified that I'll lose my vision." I could feel tears welling up and was relieved it didn't burn.

My mom's hand squeezed mine as she asked, "Would a coffee make you feel better?"

"You're asking me if a coffee would help soothe me from the

possibility that I might lose my vision. If a coffee will make me feel better about what happened? Really?" I paused before adding, "Hell yes."

Another squeeze from my mom and a giggle from Eve. She put a cup into my palm. It wasn't a standard disposable but felt like metal. I drank a big gulp.

"The new mugs came in, and I custom ordered you an extra large one." We were bantering and chatting like nothing was happening because I didn't know how to process anything yet. I just kept thinking that once the doctor came back with an answer, then I could process everything.

"You rock, Mom. Although some might say you're enabling—" I dropped the cup as a searing pain wracked my entire body. I started to seize and shake. I'm not sure what happened next, but my mom told me she panicked and tried to stop me from falling off the examination table.

The next thing I knew I was seeing the doctor, actually seeing him, almost clearly. "Hello, Helen. I have good news. Whatever was affecting your eyes seems to have been washed out with the cleaning. The swab came back clean for anything nefarious. It seemed to be a combination of acid and copper. How did that get in your eyes?"

"I don't know," I lied.

"No matter. Your blood tests showed an elevated white blood cell count. We think you may have been fighting a virus, but there are no traces of it, which means your body has fought it off."

"I'm still seeing a little blurry, and why do some things seem fuzzy, like they have an aura around them?"

"Unfortunately, whatever you got in your eye did some damage, and you'll need glasses. The halos you're seeing are part of the damage." He paused and patted me on the shoulder before continuing with: "I'm also giving you some antibiotics and some antifungal eye drops just in case whatever was in your eyes had something that didn't show up on the blood test."

"Thank you, doctor." It was all I could say. It was hard to believe what I was seeing was normal. The more I focused, the more I noticed that the auras, or halos, were only around people. The doctor was blue, my mom had a pink aura, and Eve was a beautiful gold. She looked like a painting of an angel.

Squeezing my hand again, my mom asked, "What about the seizure she had?"

"There's nothing to show why it happened, but I've made an appointment for Thursday at Timmins Mercy for an MRI, stress test, and more blood tests, just in case. Oh, I've also called Doctor Jackson, and he'll see you in about an hour for an eye test at the store." The hospital didn't have specialists; those were in the bigger hospital in Timmins.

"Thanks again," I said.

"One last thing. No drinking, no drugs, no heavy physical exercise, and absolutely no driving until we get the test results from Timmins Mercy." He also gave me a list of signs to watch out for and recommended I wear sunglasses if it was sunny.

"Well, there go my plans for tonight," I joked, but only Eve giggled.

They kept me in the hospital for a few more hours but without any more seizures and the proximity of home to the hospital, they were willing to let me go as long as someone was always with me.

As we left the hospital, my mom gave me a hug and said, "I have to head back to the diner. Are you going to be okay? I can call Jordan in early."

"Mom, I'm eighteen, I'll be fine."

"Eve volunteered to drive you to your eye appointment and to get your prescriptions. Is that okay? I could call JB if you'd rather." JB was one of two taxi drivers in Ansonville. We were related somehow, but I could never remember how.

"No, she's fine. We had a lot of fun this afternoon." Eve and I *had* had a lot of fun this afternoon, as shocking as that fact was to me.

"I'm glad to hear that," Mom said and headed out.

Everything seemed like I was looking through slightly frosted glass. It was strange for me. I'd never needed glasses before, and I was trying not to think about what had caused it. Every time I thought of the sergeant, I felt queasy.

We drove to the pharmacy first, since it was nearly closing time. It was only a few minute's drive, but the lack of conversation felt awkward. I really didn't want to think about what happened and I definitely didn't want to talk about it. Awkward or not, the silence was better.

Thankfully, the pharmacy had recently expanded its hours to eight on Saturdays. Then we headed to the small main street Jackson's Optical store. Doctor Jackson was the third Jackson to own the store and live above it.

"Thanks for seeing me after hours," I said.

In his thirties, his dark black hair was already liberally sprinkled with white. His mustache and thick rimmed glasses gave him a hipster aesthetic. "Oh, no problem. When I heard it was you, I jumped at the chance. I owe your mom for helping me out a few years back." My mom had helped him find better suppliers for his frames and helped him set up his accounting software. She loved helping people if she could. It meant that everyone in town liked her; it didn't hurt that she was a single, attractive, well-off business person.

He ran me through a series of tests and checks. At the end of the exam, he said, "You have a minus three in both eyes with a touch of astigmatism. Whatever you got into your eyes damaged the cornea and warped the eye a little." I asked him about the auras and he replied, "Side effect of the damage, it should clear up soon." He paused briefly before asking, "Did you want contacts or just glasses?"

I shrugged and Eve said, "Do you have any dailies in her prescription?" When he nodded, she said to me, "Get a month's worth and see if you like them. They're the only things I wear."

I didn't know she wore glasses and I felt bad about it. She seemed to pay attention to everything I did and I didn't even know if she wore glasses. "Okay. Do I get the glasses right away?" I asked.

He and the doctor had been clear that I wasn't allowed to wear contacts until I was fully healed.

"No, it'll take me a few days to make the lenses. I'm not too swamped, so I could make yours right away."

I went to squint at some frames and overhead him and Eve talking about how unusual it was for an optometrist to make the lenses himself. "I've got some paperwork to fill out. You choose a frame, and I'll teach you how to put in the contacts when you're better."

When he left the room, I asked, "What did the sergeant say?" I had forgotten he'd talked with her while I was being seen by the ambulance. Now that I had the medical stuff out of the way, I wanted to know what the hell happened.

In a sad whisper she said, "He threatened me. Said he'd do some terrible things to me and my aunt. It was very strange and scary."

"I'm sorry." Somehow I felt it was my fault. Eve had told me to stay in the car, and I just couldn't leave well enough alone.

"No. He was strange. He spoke without contractions and like he was having trouble breathing. The way Richard does all the time."

"That is weird." I had noticed that Richard spoke funny since last summer, but I had never heard the sergeant talk like that.

"Were his eyes always green?"

"Richard? No. The sergeant? I have no idea." *What the hell was happening?* I wondered and then remembered we needed to pick frames.

Pointing at a pair of silver and red wing tipped glasses Eve said, "What about these?"

I made a face and put on a pair or round glasses, it was her turn to make a face.

"Try these." She gave me a pair of wide lensed and thick rimmed rectangular glasses, they were a dark burgundy. I tried them on and they felt comfortable.

"How do I look?" I couldn't see clearly, but the colour went well with my hair. I had tied it back into a messy bun.

"You kind sort of have a librarian thing going on." I must have made a face because she quickly added, "A sexy librarian." I could see clearly enough to see her eyes open wide and for her to blush after saying the last part.

"If it gets you to blush this much, then I have to get them." Eve was certainly cute and I couldn't tell if she was flirting with me. It didn't feel the same as with Veronica; she was aggressive and turned me on both because it was wrong and because she was hot. Eve made me feel comfortable and loved, and that was just as much of a turn-on.

When he returned, the doctor took the frames and brought me to the back. There, he showed me the basics of putting in contacts, keeping them clean, and taking them out. He was collecting a few boxes of the dailies for me when he asked, "How's your mom?"

The old bitchier me would have told him she was too old and way out of his league, but instead I said, "Busy, but she seems to be doing well." I'm still a little bitchy but I try not to be mean to people who I respect. A list that is quite short.

"Is she dating anyone?" he asked. My mom wasn't old, she was just in her late-forties but he was in his thirties.

"I don't think so." I had no idea what else to say. This was officially awkward territory.

"I'm just curious. I saw her talking to a handsome young guy today at the diner, and they seemed chummy."

"Oh. That's kinda her job you know." Was that Harold? What does he want with my mom? And why was I feeling jealous at the idea?

On the ride home, Eve asked, "So what was that green stuff that the Sergeant threw up in your face?" She was direct but her voice was hushed.

"I have no idea, but…" I trailed off, not wanting to give word to my nightmares.

"You've seen it before, haven't you?"

My natural instincts wanted me to burst into anger at Eve's pushing, but she'd been there and she'd been threatened with a gun because of me. "I saw it this summer when Richard disappeared." I paused, took a deep breath and told her the story, "We were at the old abandoned copper mine. It has a large sand pit where we can build a giant fire, and there are a lot of caves where you can disappear for some sexy times."

Eve laughed awkwardly. "Funny way of putting it."

"I'd had a few drinks and was enjoying the fire while I waited for Richard. His sister Veronica told me she wanted to talk with me. I followed her into one of the caves and she directed me to a deep cave that had candles around a pool of what I thought was water.

"We had made out in the past and she was really into it, but that night she told me she wanted to go all the way and she was forceful." I felt ashamed for what I had done. I was worried it would make Eve hate me like everyone else did.

Eve was blushing. It was nice to be able to see clearly now, even if it felt like I had something in my eye. "Is that something you like?" Eve asked.

"I don't know. It's nice sometimes. She was always insistent that she wasn't a lesbian and this was just playing around, but that night felt different.

"I had just straddled her and had her shirt off when Richard came in. He was pissed. Called me unnatural and a two-timing bitch. He was right. I should have never messed around with his sister while dating him and not telling him. It wasn't right.

"I tried apologizing, but Veronica flew off the handle saying that he didn't understand, that what we had was true love, and he had just been keeping me warm. I got pissed and slapped her. She was drunk and would never admit we even kissed if she were sober and now she was telling me she loved me? He then charged at me and at the last minute I jumped out of the way.

"He fell into the pool. Whatever was in there was thick and green like pancake batter. The pool was only up to his knees, and we all started laughing until the sludge started climbing him. He screamed until it went into his mouth, and then he collapsed. I tried to reach for him, but Veronica held me back. Then he was gone. I called 911 and waited outside the cave but Veronica just went home. I'm still mad at her for not staying. I don't know why.

"I told the story to the police, and they said I was lying. They said we must have had a lover's spat, but Veronica told them I had attacked her and Richard had been defending her. That's why they charged me with murder.

"Richard, that asshole, waited until I was almost in jail before coming back. I was allowed to go home but under house arrest. For two weeks I got my whole life examined by a jury and questioned multiple times. If he hadn't showed up in court on the day of closing arguments, I would have been tried with second degree murder."

"Wow. That's quite the story." Eve said without any judgement in her slightly spacey tone.

"You don't believe me." My heart sank and I felt sick again.

"No, I believe you completely. It goes perfectly with what happened this afternoon."

"Thank you." That was a relief. I'd grown to really like Eve and I didn't want to lose her friendship.

It was a really quick drive home, and when we arrived at the diner, she said, "This is your stop."

"Did you want to come up and watch some movies?" The offer was out of my mouth before I had a chance to overthink it. I probably should have cried or maybe even seen a therapist, but I was trying to only deal with things when I was forced. Anyway there was only one therapist in town, and he was closed at that time.

"Absolutely. That would be awesome."

She parked behind the diner, and I could see the shape of someone in a hoodie sitting on the steps. I reached into the back seat and pulled out an aluminium baseball bat, handing it to Eve. I took my keys and put them between my knuckles like I'd seen in a movie. I was really getting tired of people waiting for me at my home.

Eve looked at the bat and shrugged saying, "Okay. I get it." She seemed a little relieved. She held the bat in one hand like a knight. She seemed pretty comfortable with it.

I got out of the car and Eve followed behind me. The light did strange things with vision. Everything seemed okay, but the arm of the person on the steps was fuzzy green.

"Who are you and what do you want?" I shouted. Squeezing my keys between my fingers.

The figure stood up and it was Veronica, but something was wrong with her face. It was blurry and green, but I could see her regular face through it like it was a weird projection. "I came to welcome you to the ONE, but you are not of the ONE." Her eyes glowed green, and she jumped the distance between us, landing on top of me. I saw Eve swing and miss her.

Veronica's weight was terrifying on my chest and hurt. I was tired of hurting. She put her hands on my face and they felt cold; so cold I thought they were going to burn my skin.

CHAPTER 5

I heard a deep metallic thud and suddenly the burning stopped. My face felt like I had frostburn on it. Veronica was now several feet away from me glaring as she rubbed her arm.

"What the hell? Veronica, what are you doing?" I yelled, wondering how she got so far away. I should have been shaken or scared, but I was just tired and angry.

"If we can not make you ONE, we will destroy you." Her face was contorted into a sneer that I could barely see under the strange green aura that was over her whole body.

Eve moved between us, swinging the baseball bat in front of her, and said, "I don't think that's a good idea." She pushed me toward the house.

"After tonight we will have the strength to do what is needed and the ONE shall rise." Her voice was jilted and mechanical like Richard's.

Fighting the sick feeling in my stomach, I laughed and said, "Make sure you watch it or it might end up collapsing." Turning to Eve, I said, "That was a soufflé joke." I was using humour to prevent myself from freaking out.

"I got it, but I'm not sure she did." She gave the bat a few more expert swings. Her voice was calm but dangerous.

Cocking her head sideways like a stray puppy, Veronica nodded and just walked away. We watched her go around the diner, and then we ran to the door, making sure it was locked before we dared go upstairs.

Inside the house, I threw my arms around Eve. "Thank you for saving me," I huffed out.

She hugged me back. She was a good hugger, not squeezing too tight or too softly. I didn't realize how cold I was until I felt her warmth.

"I need a coffee," I said. Doing something meant I didn't have to process anything yet.

Sitting at the table were my mom and Harold. He'd ditched his white shirt and jeans for a dress shirt and dress pants. He could have been a male model who'd been forced to dress at Walmart. They seemed to be having an intense conversation.

"Oh hi, honey," my mom started, but when she saw my face she turned white. "What the hell happened to your face?" I touched my cheeks and felt they were warm where Veronica had touched me. It didn't feel like a cooking burn, more like a windburn. "I'll get some burn cream," she said.

We might be a family with cooking in our genes, but so was clumsiness. We always had burn cream on hand.

Once she left the room, Harold stood and asked, "It was Richard, wasn't it?" He feigned worry, but there was a hungry look in his eyes.

"Actually, it was his sister," Eve replied, placing the bat by the front door. Harold looked at her like he was trying to complete a puzzle.

"It's spreading." His head snapped back at me and in a clinical tone he asked, "Did she spit on you?"

"Are you going to tell me who you are now? I've been attacked, puked on, almost had my eyes burned out, and was just attacked again. That's all in the past twenty-four hours. So either tell me who you are, or get out of my house."

"Did they take a swab at the hospital?"

"OUT!" I yelled.

He nodded and took his coat from next to the door. There was something heavy in its pockets. "We'll talk later," he said as he closed the door.

My mom came back just after he'd left. "Where'd Harold go?"

"He had to go do something at the hospital," Eve replied.

"Oh? I hope he's okay. He's a recruiter for U of T's cheerleading team. He said he saw you last year and really liked your form." She smiled and added, "His isn't bad either."

"Mom! Ew!" She wasn't wrong though.

I glanced into the mirror on the fridge and could see two perfect hand prints on my face. Wonderful. How the hell did someone do that? It wasn't too bad, but it didn't make any sense.

In the washroom, Mom washed off my face with some gentle soap and then put some burn cream on. It stung, but hopefully it would be healed by Monday. I quickly wondered about infection, but it didn't feel that bad. While my mom put cream on my face I told her everything that happened. She didn't say anything but she seemed worried.

With cream on my face, I made myself and Eve a coffee, then brought it to my room to drink.

"Your room is almost as messy as your car," Eve said as she sat down on my music stool.

"It's just clothes, books, and stuff, nothing really gross." Hadn't I judged Mr. Smith for being messy? At least I didn't have food everywhere.

"How are you feeling?" she asked, and there was the nose crinkle of worry again.

"Fine," I said. "Ready to party. Woo!" I deadpanned.

"I think you're deflecting with sarcasm. I don't think you should go to the big party tonight," Eve said looking worried.

"What party?" I replied with a question.

"The whole senior class is having a giant party at Roanoke. They said it's a pit mine. Steve invited me. I don't like him though, he's a jerk."

I stood up, the police had blocked off Roanoke after Richard disappeared. Said it was too dangerous. "That's the old copper mine."

"The old copper mine where you and Veronica and Richard..." she trailed off.

"Yes." I sat back and took a deep drink of coffee, enjoying the soothing taste. What does it matter if they had a party there? Whatever was going on was happening anyway, location irrelevant.

"Should we do something?" Eve sounded worried.

"What can we do?" I was feeling the fatigue of the day and the coffee wasn't helping. Everything just felt hopeless.

"I don't know. Maybe we should call the provincial police, military, or RCMP?" Eve's voice went up in pitch and she grimaced, obviously unsure.

"And tell them what? A bunch of teenagers are having a party at an old mine that has some sort of green goo, that what? What's even going on?"

"Body snatchers? Mind control? The Stuff?" Eve's face contorted into deep reflection. "Zombies?"

"Definitely not Zombies. So I'm not alone in having no idea what's going on?"

Taking my hand, she said, "You're not alone." I thought she was going to lean forward, but instead she sat up and said, "You mentioned movies? No horror movies, please."

I was thankful for the distraction. At this point I just wanted to feel warm and safe. My thoughts kept spiraling and going in wild, useless, directions.

Her hand was still on mine and I considered watching some rom-coms, but decided against it. I needed comfort, not angst.

"How about some classic Disney?" I didn't need an answer; her face lit up with excitement and relief. We both needed to do something that wasn't going to end with someone attacking me.

I set up the player and brought in a few comfy blankets before going to make popcorn. Eve went to the washroom.

As I was waiting for the popcorn to pop, my mom came in. She wasn't closing tonight. "Hey, Mom. Want to watch some movies with us?"

"Are you sure?"

Confused, I asked, "What do you mean?"

"I've seen the way she looks at you, sweetie, and I've seen how you blush when you look at her. I know you like each other."

"You think she likes me?" I asked and Mom laughed. "Um. What do you think about that?" I added tentatively.

Pulling me into a hug, Mom said, "Sweetie, it's been obvious to me since you were six that you liked boys and girls. I remember sitting you down and explaining to you that not everyone liked kissing everyone. You were so cute."

"I don't remember that." I didn't and I'd spent months thinking my mom would hate me as much as the rest of the town. I also hadn't expected her to be so accepting. I wish I had talked to her sooner. My head swam.

"Sweetie, you're eighteen and you're going off to university next year. Just be careful with this one. I know how much Richard hurt you. Also, no loud sex. Jordan is off, so I have the morning shift. Oh, and be safe. Assuming she can't get you pregnant doesn't mean she can't give you an STI." She was teasing. It was her way of showing she cared.

"Mom!" I felt my face turn bright red.

"I'm worried about you and everything that's happening. If you need anything, please ask. You know you can always go finish the year in Toronto with your father." She must have been worried if she was suggesting I go stay at Dad's. He and Nicole would be okay with it, but I really didn't want them getting all parental. They were nice in short doses.

"They have other worries and I'm sure things will get better." Neither of us believed me but I didn't feel right leaving Eve or my mom.

"Okay sweetheart, the option's there if you change your mind. And yes, I'll watch a movie with you before bed. Make me a bowl of popcorn too, please."

It felt strange to have my mom be so cavalier about my sexuality when it felt like the entire senior class thought I was a horrible person. Granted, the cheating part was bad, but that wasn't what they were angry about.

Now that I'd talked with my mom, I remembered being young and watching *Buffy the Vampire Slayer* with her. She had me watching it when I was twelve and I remembered being completely confused by the character of Willow. She was the shy, cute, bookish girl, and over the series she fell in love with the quiet guitar playing character. They had a few seasons of being awesome together, and then the show moved to college.

In college, she met a girl and they became close. The writers used witchcraft as a blatant analogy for being gay. The two fell in love; they were cute together and happy.

What had confused me was how once she'd started dating the girl, Willow didn't like boys anymore. She's been open about finding boys attractive and was attracted to her boyfriend at the time but no more. From that point on she was purely a lesbian. It made me think that liking girls and boys was strange or wrong.

"*Meet the Robinsons*," Mom suggested as I walked in with three bowls of popcorn.

"No. Something about a crazed hat controlling people's minds doesn't sound good to me."

"*Aladdin*?" suggested Eve.

We watched *Aladdin* and then *Frozen*, then my mom went to bed. We'd been sitting with a cushion between us during the first two movies, and as we started *Snow White*, I put my hand on hers. I felt silly as a shock of excitement shot up my arm. Her hands were soft and strong. They were warm and smooth which helped calm my frayed nerves.

We held hands until she fell asleep. I helped lay her down on the couch, made another coffee and went to my room. I could see the couch from my desk chair and I pulled out my guitar. She was beautiful, a purple classic Les Paul electric. Long, elegant, and curvy, just like me. I'd made that comment to Veronica when we jammed, and she'd gotten really uncomfortable. At the time, I thought it was because she didn't like comparing guitars to people, but now I know it's because she liked me.

I plugged my headphones into the amp and then the guitar and turned it on. I probably should have tuned it, but it still sounded good. I love my violin and I'm way better at it, but there's a sense of power the electric has that the violin doesn't. I'd considered saving money for a fancy electric violin, but they weren't cheap. Maybe I could hint to my dad about it.

Playing some scales to warm up, I then played some Disney songs to stay on theme. Playing "Let It Go" with the overdrive on was awesome. It's more cathartic when you can sing, but I didn't want to wake anyone up.

When my fingers hurt, I stopped and tried to watch another movie. Unfortunately, no matter how much coffee I drank, I still had to sleep. I was woken up by Eve pushing on my shoulder and saying, "Wake up, Helen."

"I'm up. What time is it?"

"It's six in the morning. You were making little alarmed noises and whimpering in your sleep."

"Oh. I'm sorry. I should have warned you. Go back to sleep. I'll make myself a coffee and do some homework."

Making a face that said she thought I was being ridiculous, she asked, "You're getting up? But you only slept a few hours."

"More than enough."

"Did you have a nightmare? Is that what happened?" She put both hands to her mouth in comic surprise and added, "It's from this summer isn't it? That's why you drink so much coffee, so you don't have to sleep." She hugged me and added, "I'm so sorry."

Again, my anger flared and I wanted to tell her to keep her pity to herself, but I didn't. Her hug sent soothing warmth coursing through my body. The kind of warmth you get from affection, not just attraction. She told me she was sorry again and went back to sleep. I made a coffee and worked on some homework.

Mom had already gone downstairs by the time I'd woken up, so it was just me and Eve in the house when the doorbell rang. She must have been tired because she didn't wake up.

I looked out the window and was surprised to see a priest at the door dressed all in black with his white collar. He was in his fifties with silver hair and held himself with confidence. His eyes were grey which was a relief. I wouldn't have opened the door for someone with green eyes.

"I'm Father Williams with Saint Marie's church."

"Hello, Father. How may I help you?" I assumed he wanted a donation or something.

"It's I who can help you, my child." I didn't like the sound of that. "May I come in?"

Taking a deep breath and trying not to sigh, I invited him in. I wanted to be polite. It wasn't his fault he was here.

Once in the kitchen, I asked if he'd like a coffee. When he said yes, I made it and gave it to him. I felt a little uncomfortable in my comfy superhero pyjamas, but he didn't say anything about it.

"I have a member of my congregation that has admitted to sinful actions with you." That's when it hit me that Richard and Veronica went to Saint Marie's.

"Oh?" I asked, trying not to seem panicked.

"It's alright child. We all face temptation at times, for some it's gluttony, for others it's lust." I was starting to see where things were going and my coffee cup wasn't big enough to hide behind. "Your urges are a test, but you must be strong and not give in to them. You must find solace in Jesus and know that laying with another woman will ensure your place in hell."

If I hadn't had the conversation with my mom the night before, I might have burst into tears. I was tempted as it was, but instead I said, "I appreciate your interest in my soul, Father. I have discussed this with my minister Father Michael." My anger was rising and I was really close to telling this priest off, the hell with my soul... literally, I guess.

"Oh." He scowled. I didn't think I'd ever seen such a deep frown. "The Anglican Church has made a dire mistake in allowing deviant and sinful behaviour in its temples."

I had no idea what to say, so we stared at each other awkwardly for a few moments until Eve sauntered in with her shirt on inside out, "Helen, are you coming back to bed?" she said it in a breathy deep voice that made my stomach feel like mush. My anger evaporated.

The priest's eyes opened wide and he stood up and left without another word. Eve and I burst into laughter when the door closed behind him.

"Is that what you do for fun on Sundays? Freak out priests? 'Cause that was fun," Eve said between laughs.

"No, this seems to be a new thing. Someone at school is telling the clergy that I'm having lots and lots of gay sex."

Eve waited for a little while then she said, "That sounds like a terrible prank to pull on someone."

"Agreed, and it's really awkward. I'm not having *any* sex." I sighed dramatically and drained my coffee.

Looking at the clock on the stove, Eve's face fell, and she said, "Speaking of clergy, I need to get back to my aunt's house to change and get ready for church." I gave her a surprised look. I hadn't pegged her as a religious person. "My aunt insists I go with her as a condition of living with her."

"I hope it's not Saint Marie's. Knowing your aunt, that makes sense. Take my car to get back into town. Can you pick me up for school tomorrow morning?" I suggested, hoping she'd want to come back this afternoon.

"Alright," she said in her calm, spacey way and went to the bathroom. When she came out, her clothes were back on properly and she'd tamed her golden hair. I so wanted to run my hands through it, but something stopped me.

I walked her to the door and she said, "Thank you." I started to lean forward for a hug, but she didn't notice and left. I wasn't sure how to take that. We'd been sort of on a full day date with weird events in between. Had I misread her? Did she not want to be with me?

Standing there trying to understand what was going on, I should have gone back in and closed the door. Instead I watched her drive off, trying to understand what was going on between us and more importantly, what I wanted.

"I'm ready to tell you who I am and what I'm doing here." Harold appeared around the corner of the house making me jump. "Sorry, I didn't mean to scare you. Is everything okay between you and your girlfriend?"

"None of your business," I answered instinctively. My hand was around the baseball bat behind the door frame.

"Okay. I just thought, you know. Can I buy you a coffee and we'll talk?" His amber eyes were squinting in worry and his smile was tight, but he was still handsome. I reassessed how old I thought he was. Originally, I thought he was in his thirties but now, his worry showed a lack of lines, and I was fairly certain he was in his mid-twenties. Somehow that made him feel more attainable.

"My mom owns the place. I get free coffee."

"I'll buy you a Timmies then?" He smiled. His eyes gave away his cocky confidence and that he wasn't anything like Richard.

I did not want to be alone in the apartment. The idea of it made my heart pound a little too fast. "Fine. Let me change and I'll be out in ten minutes." I closed the door before he could ask if he could come in. That didn't sound safe, and I wasn't going to be alone with someone I didn't know.

Being annoyed with Eve wasn't fair to her but I was annoyed, and the vindictive part of me wanted revenge. That made my choice of clothing easy. I wore a light green sweater with a scandalously low neckline. I don't have a lot of cleavage so I paired it with my best push up bra, and then a pair of tight black jeans. With my white boots and coat, I'd be hot. I hoped.

I was excited to see how he'd react, and I was disappointed when he didn't. He just nodded and we started walking. The Tim Hortons wasn't far. I wouldn't have agreed if I needed a ride to get back or things went weird, which they'd been doing a lot lately.

I still didn't like being alone with him, but it was still better than being alone at home.

There was nothing but car engines and awkward silence. That was odd. Normally there were at least some crows or other birds. "This quiet is weird," I said, hoping to break the awkwardness.

"I just thought it would be simpler to talk in a building than the side of the street."

"I mean there's no birds, dogs, or bugs."

He stopped and went toward the ditch on the side of the road. He pulled out a small vial and some plastic gloves from his long leather coat and took a sample of the water and the dirt. He then stared at the farmers field as if expecting it to get up and dance away.

I enjoyed the sight of him bending over and tried not to be obvious about it. He had a blue aura, like the doctor, optometrist, and priest. It seemed most people had a blue aura.

"Uh, can we keep going?" I asked after a few minutes of more samples and staring. He said nothing about it and didn't bring up the silence again.

At the Timmies, he bought us each a coffee. We sipped it, and he made a face before saying, "I've had your mother's coffee for less than a week and now I can't stand this stuff anymore."

"It's the cocaine she puts in it," I joked.

His eyes grew wide before he understood and laughed. "Seriously, why is her coffee so different even from the other small roasters?"

The Timmies had a dozen other patrons but mostly the drive-through was busy. It smelled of coffee and donuts. Even the cold plastic chairs didn't dim its warmth.

This wasn't the first time an attractive person had taken me out to ask about my mother's secret. A representative from a big coffee company from Seattle had taken me out for a lobster dinner when my mom had opened distribution across Ontario and Quebec.

"My mom travelled when she was young and she studied food and coffee from all over the world. She says she studied with a shaman in Ethiopia that showed her how to roast the beans in a way we don't. She even commissioned a special custom roaster from a local metal shop."

Cocking his eyebrow in disbelief, he said, "A shaman, eh?"

"She says that coffee has great ability to heal both body and spirit, but only if it's roasted and brewed in a special way."

"I'd love to see her methods."

It was my turn to laugh. "So would lots of people. Even *I'm* not allowed in the roasting room."

I thought he was going to say something, but he must have changed his mind because he took a deep drink of his coffee.

We sat there until I finally cracked and asked, "So who are you and what do you want?"

"Straight to the point," he said and nodded. He wiggled like he was uncomfortable, like someone doing something they weren't sure was right.

"This will be hard to believe but I'm a scientist with a top-secret organization. We monitor weird and unusual things."

"So you're Fox Mulder?"

"No, not aliens." He shook his head in disgust before continuing, "There is a lot more in nature that is weird and dangerous that isn't aliens."

"Thanks Hamlet." When his face furrowed in confusion, I quoted, "'There are more things in heaven and earth, Horatio, Than are dreamed of in your philosophy.' It's Shakespeare."

"This isn't fiction, Helen. Something horrible is going on in Ansonville, and I think it's happened before."

CHAPTER 6

"Oooh scary! Very seasonal of you," I snarked. I already knew something weird was going on in town. I didn't need his vague warnings.

"I'm serious," he said, completely dejected. He suddenly seemed older and much more tired than he'd been a few seconds before.

"Fine. I sort of figured something weird was going on. What's your full name and rank?"

"How did you know I had a rank?"

"No one has a body like that by spending all day in the lab." My complimenting his body made him blush.

"Second lieutenant Harold Harnel, Elmsley Science Corps." He seemed proud, but it was just a bunch of words to me.

"I had an English teacher called Harnel. Any relation?"

"You're not taking this seriously," he said and started to stand up.

I reached out and touched his hand, and he sat back down. I sighed and said, "It's easier to joke than to think about this. For you, it's a case or whatever, for me it's my life, and it hurts." Literally, my face still stung from Veronica's hands.

The raised eyebrow and grimace told me he didn't believe me. So I told him everything that had happened from the beginning. He pulled out a notebook and wrote down what I said, adding little notes on the side. After I was done, he asked, "Is it possible that Richard and Veronica had these powers before?"

"I think I would have noticed if my ex-boyfriend and his sister had been weird freaks of nature."

"Probably not, but we can't exclude the possibility." He stopped and stared straight at me, blushing before asking in a whisper, "You had a boyfriend? Aren't you and the pretty blonde girl together?"

Leaning over with a confidence I didn't feel, I said, "It's possible to like both." Inside, my heart was beating way too fast.

"Oh. I guess it is." He paused and finally said, "I need to see that cave."

It was obvious that he wanted me to take him, but there was no way I was going back there. "Good luck. I'll draw you a map." I pulled out a pen and a piece of paper from my purse and started sketching a quick map of where the cave was.

Taking my hand in his, he said, "It would be a lot easier if you went with me."

"Maybe for you, but I really don't want to risk it."

There was a long silence before he said, "Okay. I'll walk you home."

Normally I would have scoffed at someone offering to walk me home, but after the past few days, I didn't want to take the chance of being ambushed at my door. Again.

It seemed like he was thinking deeply and between that and the road noise he didn't say anything.

When we finally arrived at my door, he sort of shuffled there and asked, "So does this mean that you and the blonde girl aren't together?"

Between the weird and everything else that had happened, I was feeling lonely and craving human touch. It had been over three months since I'd kissed someone, and call me what you want, I like kissing. I grabbed him by the shoulders and pushed him against the brick façade next to the door. His mouth tasted of aspartame sweetened coffee and his lips were soft against mine.

For a sexy-military-geek, I'd expected him to be a better kisser. What he lacked in technique, he made up for in enthusiasm though, and he learned quickly.

My lips were starting to feel deliciously raw when I heard someone clearing their throat next to me. My mother was standing with a woman in a full nun's outfit. I failed to suppress a laugh and said, "Hi, Mom."

"Who's this?" she asked, despite having met him before. I think it was more shorthand for who is this to you.

"This is Harold. He's new in town doing research on the old copper mine." At the mention of the mine, my mother's face went white.

We all just stood there until I said, "Harold, let me know how the tests go." I tried to sound like I was saying goodbye and it must have worked because he left. I turned to the nun and said, "I'm not sure what you've been told and I know that looked bad, but I've been counselled by a priest and a minister already. Thank you, but I don't need a repeat."

Both the nun and my mom burst out laughing. I stared at them shocked and couldn't figure out what was going on.

"This isn't a nun, sweetie. It's just Rolande." I had mistaken my mom's oldest friend and honorary aunt as a nun. I felt like an idiot. She lived on a farm just out of town. The Lacombe farm had been in her family for decades.

"Hey kid. So you've been approached by a priest and a minister about sex? You're missing an imam and a rabbi for a bad joke."

Shaking my head, I laughed. My mom told Rolande to head into the diner and my mom would join her. When her friend was out of the way, she said "Helen Camille Benson. What the hell is going on? First, you date the popular boy and go all *Mean Girls*. You break up, and I think you start dating a nice young lady, and now you're making out with some sort of military scientist who was pretending to be a cheer scout?"

"How did you know he's military? I thought he told you he was a cheer scout?"

"You don't get a body like that working in a lab and you don't get chemical burn scars on your wrists from cheer. And you're changing the subject." She didn't sound happy. I was impressed with how observant she was. Maybe it was from her travels or from being in business for twenty years.

It wasn't a conversation I wanted to have at our front door, or ever. "What do you want, Mom? Eve is cute, but I don't think she wants me in that way. Harold is... Well you saw him..." I trailed off not knowing what to say.

"I did." Her eyes focused at the distance and grimaced. "Sweetie, I'm worried about you. You've been all over the place since the whole Richard thing, and I don't want you making mistakes or rushing things just because he's cute."

"Mom, I'm not going to sleep with Harold. Nor am I rushing anything. It was just a kiss."

"Just be careful, both physically and emotionally."

"I'll try."

She nodded and headed toward the diner. I headed upstairs to make myself a *real* coffee.

I sat at the coffee table randomly browsing my social media, but not reading it. Most of the ads had half naked men and women and a lot of the posts had girls from my high school shaming others for what they wore, did, or said. From one part of society, I was being told sex was awesome and to be sexy, but from the other side, I was being told that my body was a temple and women shouldn't have or like sex.

It was overwhelming. I felt like there must be something wrong with me for being attracted to anyone, let alone almost everyone. I turned on the incognito function on my browser and searched for *Why am I so horny*. The results surprised me. They were mostly about women, which I hadn't expected, and they mostly dealt with pseudoscience. Lots of talk about foods and spiritual stuff.

It all read like bullshit to me, and I didn't have the energy to wade through the muck of it.

I closed the browser and a chat head popped up.

"Hey cuz. What's up?" Bart was my cousin on my Dad's side. He was huge and built like a brick, which is what people liked to call him.

"Hey Barty. Things are good."

"Really? I don't believe you."

"Things are weird and I'm not sure what's going on."

"This is about a guy or girl. Tell me it's not that jackass ex of yours. I swear I'll drive up there and beat the crap out of you if you're dating him again."

Despite myself, I laughed. Bart likes to talk about beating people up, but he's a giant teddy bear. "Right. Like you could."

"You're avoiding the question."

"Fine, yes it's about a girl and a boy." Bart was the only one I'd told everything to when it happened. He'd listened instead of arguing or judging. When he didn't say anything, I added, "They're both hot, but I'm not sure if they're really into me or— why do I crave kissing them?"

He put the little blush emoji and added, "It's completely okay to be horny. Some people always are, some never are, that's just life."

"That's great, but what do I do about it?"

"Um. I'm not sure I want to get into details, but there's this thing on the end of your arm called a hand and the fingers are really useful for relieving stress."

Almost spitting out my coffee, I said, "Masturbation! It's called masturbation." I wished I could see his face, it was probably redder than either of our hair.

"Yes, that's it." He didn't say anything for a while before adding, "Seriously, though. If you like them, tell them. Don't waste a bunch of time pining away when you could be kissing." *The way I did.* That last part wasn't written, but definitely hung in the air.

Bart had a crush on this girl Francine, and it took her being kidnapped and disappearing for him to tell her how he felt. Turns out she felt the same way, and they could have been together the whole time.

"Thanks. Sometimes it's easy to get stuck in my own head."

"No problem, and hey, if you came to Baker U, I could give you this advice all the time in person." He'd been on me for the past two years to go to his home town university. Baker University was world-renowned in social sciences, but only okay in real science. He'd only gotten worse since the beginning of the semester. He was loving it there.

"I said I'd think about it. Applications are next month."

"Alright. I got to go. Francine is here, and we're going to the movies."

"Bye Barty."

"Bye Hel!"

Wanting both to be around people and by myself I texted Eve, "Hey." I shook my head. I was truly a master of the English language.

I didn't have to wait long before she replied to me, "Hi. I'm just finishing some chores. Wanna meet up?" It was followed by a smiley emoji.

"Awesome," was all I replied.

"Pick you up in twenty," she texted, followed by a kiss emoji.

Arg! What the hell was I doing, crushing on the new kid and kissing the sexy stalker?

Gently banging my head against my wall, I didn't hear my mom coming in. She turned the corner into my room and said, "If you want to take down that wall, I can get you a sledge hammer."

"I thought you were hanging out with Aunt Rolande?"

"I was. It's been two hours. Is this what you do when you're alone? 'Cause I hear masturbation is more fun than giving yourself a concussion." She tried not laughing, but couldn't contain her smile.

"Mom, you're as bad as Bart! I'm going to hang out with Eve. Is that okay?"

"Well, your cousin is a smart cookie. You know you don't need my permission." She walked into the room and pulled me off my chair into a hug. She smelled slightly of oil and spices. "Just be safe."

Squirming out of the hug, I said, "Thanks, Mom." When her brow furrowed, I added, "For accepting me the way I am."

"Accepting you as you are is the easy job. You have the hard one: accepting yourself."

After the hug, I hurried to get ready, not that I had much to do. Then I waited. I hated not driving. The freedom to go wherever I wanted had been the only control I had for the past year and having it taken away was frustrating.

The first thing Eve asked when she arrived was: "Where should we go?"

"How do you feel about running away and joining the circus?"

Pensively, Eve considered the question and said, "I don't like how older ones treat animals, and I think Cirque du Soleil requires a high school diploma."

"I was joking." I couldn't help but smile. The afternoon sun was reflecting through her hair, and she smelled vaguely of cherries. My eyes were having issues focussing in the light and that made her seem even more angelic. It took everything I had not to lean over and kiss her.

"Oh," she said blushing. "Maybe we could go see a movie?"

"Sure. Old man Daniels' Cinema only plays old movies though."

"Are we talking classic black and white or last month's blockbusters?"

"Depends how he's feeling. He doesn't tell anyone until the day of. Let's drive by and see."

Old man Daniels must have been in a sappy mood because the day's movies were all animations or love stories. We had twenty minutes before the next set started. With only two cinemas, we had the choice between *Amelie* and *Shrek*.

"Yay! I love *Amelie*," Eve said as she parked the car.

"Great, you get the tickets, and I'll get the popcorn."

The cinema was modelled after the old cinemas that you see in television and movies. The box office was at the front and there was a small concession stand as you came in. From there, there were ushers at the doors of each cinema who would take your ticket.

I passed the box office and got in line for popcorn. Old man Daniels had a secret recipe for his popcorn that made it the best I've ever tasted. Because of that, people would come buy the popcorn even if they weren't going to the movie. The line wasn't long, but at the head of it was Dean. He might have taken an entire bottle of oil and dumped it in his hair.

To my shock, next to him was Veronica. The bright light from outside with the darker cinema lights were playing tricks with my eyes; she still was kinda fuzzy and like someone had put a weird green filter on her. It was the same as when attacked me but worse, as if her entire body and her clothes were turning green.

Turning to Veronica, Dean said something. Veronica took a step back and slapped him. I don't like Dean, he's creepy, but I don't generally want him hurt. That slap, however, made me enormously happy. Like something was still normal in this weird town.

Chuckling to himself, Dean walked past me and into the cinema playing *Shrek*. I noticed he had a pink aura, like my mom's. Veronica, however, saw me, and after taking her popcorn, she stomped directly toward me, glaring. She stopped and looked me in the eye. Only the velvet rope stood between us, and I was terrified. Her eyes were a dirty green that seemed to glow. Was it just my vision problems?

"You'll be ONE!" she said heading for *Shrek*.

She went into Shrek and I laughed, saying, "She wasn't an ogre until I kissed her."

Those around me in line pretended not to know me. I glanced around self-consciously and saw Steve glaring at me. His skin had the same fuzzy green filter as Veronica's, except unlike her, he wasn't covered. It was splotchy like a dalmatian's spots.

I bought a large bag of popcorn, some M&M's, and two iced teas. Steve's eyes followed me.

"Why is the hockey jock staring at you like you're something stuck to his shoe?" Eve came up behind me and took one of the drinks. She put a gentle hand on my arm as we found our seats.

"I'm not sure. Does he seem different to you?"

"Not really. Did he always have green eyes?"

Sighing with a little relief, I said, "No. And now I'm worried."

The cinema was shockingly empty. I knew that French language films weren't popular here, but *Amelie* was a classic and I'd expected more than the half-dozen people watching with us.

"I half expected you to get coffee," she said with a smirk that made my insides jelly.

"I don't *only* drink coffee." I fake pouted before adding, "Besides, they don't have any." We both laughed, and she put her hand on my leg. I could feel her heat through my jeans.

"I think something bad is going on, and I'm worried about you." Her words were quick and nervous, not her normal soft spacey tone.

"I like you and I kissed Harold because I thought you didn't like me, but now I don't know and all I want to do is kiss you." I looked away feeling myself blush. Bart said to be honest, I just wish I could have been cool about it.

"Oh. I was talking about the green eyes and the fact that your ex-boyfriend is puking green stuff at you," she replied, her tone soft.

"Okay. Um. Yeah. Let's talk about that."

Putting her hand on my cheek and gently turning my gaze to her, she said, "I think it has to do with the mine." Cocking her head, she said, "Who's Harold?"

"I'm not going back there. And he's the James Dean impersonator military guy." My voice wobbled as she gently took her hand off my cheek.

"I understand, but maybe it would help with your nightmares if you faced it. You said he was handsome, so it makes sense you'd want to kiss him." Her eyes narrowed.

"Why are we having two conversations at once? It's confusing. I'll go with you if you insist, but only because it's you, and I kissed him because I wanted to kiss you, but you just left this morning."

"I had to go to church." Her head moved closer to mine.

"I hoped for a hug or..." Our lips came closer.

"I didn't know if you liked me. You're sometimes hard to read through the sarcasm and sass."

"I'm never sarcastic," I joked, our lips almost touching.

A loud crash echoed in the cinema as a seat broke through the wall only missing us by a few centimetres.

The kiss didn't happen, since we threw ourselves to the ground to avoid the next set of seats crashing through the wall.

Chapter 7

The air was thick with dust and people were screaming. All I could think about was how nice it was to have Eve on top of me. She must have thrown herself on me to protect me. How chivalrous.

Something roared, and I gently pushed on Eve. We both got up enough to see over our seat. Through the haze of dust, Dean was running toward the emergency exit at the front of the cinema. Others were running the same way and some were running for the entrance.

The massive hole in the cinder brick wall showed that the other cinema was emptying faster but with more people, some getting trampled. Only two people weren't moving away, Richard and Veronica.

Both appeared fuzzy and green. Richard roared again. Every vein I could see was throbbing, and I couldn't help but think of the Hulk. He saw me and his eyes glowed green. He stalked toward us, punched one of the exposed bricks, and it crumbled like it was made of cake.

"We should probably get out of here." Eve sounded, understandably, panicked.

Moving faster than I thought possible, Richard was in front of me by the time I stood up. "You are an aberration." His words sounded mechanical but still filled with loathing.

"Says the guy with glowing eyes who can punch through walls." Apparently I'm incapable of turning off my sass, even when I should.

He raised his arm, and I expected him to hit me. He'd hit me once, when he'd flown into a jealous rage because he said I was flirting with Steve. I'd kicked him in the balls and then kneed him in the nose. It's amazing what breaking a boy's nose does for his respect levels.

Something told me I wouldn't be able to get away with that trick with the new and creepier Richard.

Before he hit me, Veronica was next to him holding his arm in place. "There are not enough of them who are of the ONE." Yes, I could hear the all-caps on that one word again. "Terminating her will attract attention."

A low growl escaped his throat as he turned away. I held my tongue until they'd gotten to the emergency exit. "'Cause a great big hole in the local cinema doesn't attract attention." Eve hugged me, and I could tell she was shaking. I held her and stroked her hair.

Letting myself enjoy the warmth of her body, I tried not to think any sexy thoughts. Apparently stress makes me sassy and horny. I swore and said, "There's dirt in our popcorn."

Pulling away, Eve laughed.

As we left the building, Sergeant Bannerman pulled up with an ambulance and two other officers.

"Okay folks. There's been some structural damage to the cinema, and I need everyone to move to the other side of the street."

As I passed by him, I grimaced and said to Eve, "Yeah, that's what it is."

He smirked at me and patted his gun.

In the car, I started shaking uncontrollably. I'd had a bad couple of days and being subtly threatened was the last straw.

"Are you okay? You're a little green." Eve's face was scrunched up in concern.

"I'm f—" I started but decided I wasn't. "I don't feel so good." The world started bending and I couldn't decide whether I was walking or falling.

I know I got to the car, but I don't remember the ride. All I remember is a dark blanket of green trying to smother me and then the world went black.

I woke up in my own bed with a massive headache. I almost never got headaches before this summer. I tried to sit up, but a strong warm hand stopped me.

"Sweetie, your temperature is really low. Don't move. I'll get you a warm drink."

From a distance I heard mom and Eve talking.

"I'm sorry, Ms. Benson, but we only went to the movies."

"She's nearly hypothermic. It's only five degrees outside; this shouldn't be happening."

I could hear mom grinding coffee beans, and I concentrated on the only spot on the ceiling that wasn't spinning.

They said I was almost hypothermic, but I felt warm. The smell of coffee normally made me feel better, but this time it turned my stomach.

Everything stopped for a moment and my mind, vision, and thoughts turned green. I felt like I was connected to something. There were thoughts and visions in my head that weren't my own.

The room disappeared, and I could see Harold. Everything was green and hazy but I was in some sort of puddle. His hands shook nervously holding a little jar, the same kind he used to get the dirt from the side of the road earlier that day.

Fire exploded into my mouth, bitter and too sweet at the same time. It set my body aflame as I was pulled back into my body. I lost connection to the Green, and it felt like losing a part of myself.

I screamed and then started to shiver uncontrollably. I heard my mom say, "It's not enough. You're going to have to do something."

"What? I'm—"

Mom cut her off with, "I know what you are and I know you have some sort of abilities. You've used them before, now help her."

The burning and shivering stopped, and I started to feel comfortably warm. As I opened my eyes, I could have sworn I saw Eve's glow get more intense.

"What happened?" I asked, the odd dreams fading a little.

Eve looked at my mom who said, "You've had an intense couple of days, and your body gave out. You need to rest." Holding up her hand to stop me, she added, "No arguing. A day on the couch being taken care of will make you feel better."

I took the coffee from the side table and drank some; it no longer smelled wrong. It was a warm hug in my mouth, and I sighed at how much better it made me feel.

"Fine. Let's watch *Amelie* with a big bowl of popcorn," I said to Eve.

"Wait. You own the movie? Why would you go out if we could have watched it here?"

I was still weak, so I gestured for her to help me up. I was surprised that despite her short stoutness she was strong.

Once I was up, I said, "It's the experience. Sharing a movie with a crowd, holding someone's hand, being away from distractions. It's just…" I trailed off as we got to the couch, and I sat down heavily. I was still really dizzy and gravity was doing weird things.

"I understand. It's a communal experience."

"Yeah, and they make awesome popcorn." I sighed. Everything felt too bright. I took another sip of coffee.

"Your mother is an excellent cook. Could she not replicate the recipe?" She sat on the edge of the couch and peered at me through her too-blue eyes, confused and amused at the same time.

"Probably. Mom doesn't like to compete with others in town. She never does something niche if someone's already done it. That's why she doesn't make desserts."

"Ah. That's honourable of her. I will go ask her to make some."

There was something about Eve that seemed tired, like she'd spent the day moving someone. I wondered if the past few days had been wearing on her. I felt bad and then I felt angry.

I'd found someone I liked, who liked me and who wasn't a jerk, and all this bullshit was going on. How desperately unfair.

I must have fallen asleep in my righteous anger because the next thing I knew I had a blanket and a giant bowl of popcorn on my lap. "I fell asleep again, didn't I?"

Looking up from her phone, Eve said, "Yes, but it's okay. I wanted to tell my aunt I was going to be home late tonight anyway."

Cocking an eyebrow, I said, "Oh? That's presumptuous."

For a quick second she panicked, wide eyed and all, then she saw my smile and stuck out her tongue. "Your Mom invited me to dinner. Said it was a big breakfast kind of dinner."

Raising my voice, I screamed, "I love you, Mom!"

Her reply from the kitchen was, "Fine, I'll make the apple cinnamon pancakes."

"You know, you're quite odd," Eve said, and the way her eyes studied me as she spoke sent shivers up and down my spine. I guess I was feeling better.

Mondays are terrible in general. I didn't used to think so, back when I was popular. This Monday was particularly crappy. I brought Mr. Smith his coffee, and as I was heading to my first class, I passed Veronica, Amanda, Lindsay, and Lacey. They were all in dance and the band with me, and I'd considered them my best friends. I braced myself for the usual hateful words or mocking. They didn't even acknowledge me as they passed. Their matching green eyes just stared right ahead. Maybe they'd gotten coloured contacts? That would make way more sense than whatever was actually going on here. I watched them go and scrunched my eyes. They all had that fuzzy distortion filter on them, just like Steve had the day before.

If I thought that was disconcerting, class was a million times more. The majority of the class just stared ahead and said nothing. After my second class, I met Eve at her locker and asked, "Have you noticed anything strange in your classes?"

"Nope."

"Nothing?"

"Oh, you mean how everyone seems to have green eyes and stares blankly ahead like bad robot replicants?" She smiled, concern crinkling her forehead in the most adorable way.

I kissed her forehead. She was just so cute, and it was on the right height level. "Yes, that."

"It's everyone who went to the party on Saturday."

I nodded and took her hand. "Can I sit with you at lunch?"

"Yes. Yes. Yes!" she mockingly replied, pretending I'd just proposed. She fanned her face and added, "I've always dreamed of this day."

I hugged her then and did my best not to cry. "You're awesome."

"Did I do the right level of silly?"

A group of tenth graders passed by and I heard one of them say, "Gay!" and another "Hot!" At least that meant they weren't green eyed zombies.

"Jealous much?" I said after them. They snickered and walked away faster.

I was glad to avoid the cafeteria at lunch. Eve was cute and talked about random things, like she was trying to distract me.

Back at the school, as I headed toward biochem, Mr. Smith stopped me by his office. "Miss Benson, may I have a word?"

I swallowed my "No," and said, "Did I forget your order? I'm going to my teleconference course," which was my way of saying I didn't want to.

"No, I didn't make one. It will only take a moment." It was his way of saying I didn't have a choice.

In his office, I tried not to take in the mess. How does someone in 2015 use so much paper?

"I've had some complaints about your behaviour."

"Okay?" I wanted to say something snarky, but for the first time in a while I hadn't been particularly bitchy that day. Between Eve and all the weird things going on, I just sort of went through my day hoping for it to end.

"I've been told you're acting inappropriately with Miss Swan."

It took me a few seconds to remember who Miss Swan was, and then a few more to catch what he was saying. "What have we done?" I asked before I got too angry.

"Most of the students here are innocent, and they don't want your lifestyle on full display."

"My lifestyle? Today, I hugged a girl, kissed her forehead, and held her hand. Is that what you're considering inappropriate?" I was trying hard not to scream.

"Miss Benson, there's no reason to get antagonistic. I'm just asking you to tone it down a little."

Standing up, I found I was shaking, the world around me went green. I took a deep breath and a drink of my coffee before saying, "This town can take its homophobia and choke on it." He opened his mouth to say something but I cut him off, "You, however, are an educator and a person in authority. Start acting like it and dismiss these 'complaints' for the bullshit that they are."

"Miss Benson!" he said reproachfully.

"No, Mr. Smith. You're going to dismiss these complaints, and I'm not going to contact the school board about you encouraging hate based on sexuality in the school. Not to mention Miss Swan's aunt might want to know about the atmosphere you are harbouring here."

Eyes wide and panicky, his mouth opened and closed a few times before stopping and taking a deep gulp of air. "I'm sorry for wasting your time. However, I still recommend you temper your actions around the other students. They might not all complain to me." *They might take actions into their own hands,* was the part he didn't want to say out loud.

Leaving, I saw Miss Lacroix hunting for someone to preach to and took another path. I walked so fast to biochemistry that I didn't even notice the smell of old cigarettes on Dean until class was well underway.

"You look pissed," Dean said while we had some time to work in class.

"I am."

"Considering the hot chick you're dating, I'm surprised."

"We're not dating, we're just. I don't know. Are you going to call me names now?"

"Why? 'Cause you're dating a girl? Who cares? You guys are hot. I'd much rather watch you and her mush faces than you and Richard."

"Thanks for not being a total dick."

"Har har, like I haven't heard that one a million times. If you two need some dick in your lives I'm okay with a threesome." He waggled his eyebrows theatrically.

"Yeah, there it is." I smirked at him, and he suddenly became serious.

"Hey. I'm having a party at my place on Friday. You and Eve should come by."

"Are other people invited?"

"Yeah, a bunch of others. It's a costume party so dress slutty."

"Why not on Saturday?"

"I'm taking my sister trick or treating," he said, his eyes pleading with me not to tease him.

"Cool. We might come. There's no smoking indoors is there?" He shook his head and rolled his eyes.

When had I started liking Dean more than most of the senior class? He was an arrogant smelly ass, but I was starting to think he was a decent guy under the propositions and smoke.

Class was about variable toxicity and how it affects, or stresses, living cells. I was fascinated by the idea that two organisms could be affected completely differently by the same toxin. Dose, metabolism, and environment had such a large impact that some organisms could survive something that should kill them simply because of their diet.

"That's so cool," I said at the end.

"Yeah but I liked the module on parasites better." Dean smirked.

"You just liked the zombie ants." We had studied ants that get infected by a parasitic fungus that turned them into zombies with no goal but to spread the infection. The group of ants that were not affected would try and get rid of the infected ants, but eventually the infected exploded and spread the infection. It was terrifying.

"Yeah! And disgusting." Dean paused and then glanced around nervously. "Feels a little on the nose lately though." Before he could explain, he left. His swagger seemed a little diminished by his jumpiness.

"Can I walk you to your class?" A hand like ice gripped my arm and pulled me toward my next class. The hand radiated cold like being touched by a freezer.

"What do you want, Veronica? You've made it clear it's not me." It was meant as sass, but the emotion behind it was too real. I had really liked her before all this.

"Don't think we have forgotten about you simply because we ignored you today. When we're ready, you'll be part of the ONE."

"Yes yes. The One. I get it. Let go." I threw my weight down and spun into a kick, tripping Veronica and forcing her to release me despite her freakish strength and cold.

The rest of the day was an exercise in patience, and I didn't have any left. My arm hurt, my head hurt, and I was overall grumpy.

When I met up with Eve at my car, I was in quite the mood. I wanted to hit someone or— Actually, I just wanted to hit someone.

"Let's get the hell out of here." I sighed loudly. I was in such a bad mood that I didn't notice the extremely attractive redhead talking to Eve.

The woman was maybe in her twenties and was flawless in every way. It was almost painful how pretty she was. Then she smiled at me, and I could have sworn her canine teeth were longer than they should be.

"Hello, Miss Benson. I'm looking for my partner, and I was told you may have been seen with him?" She held up a badge and a picture of her and Harold in military uniforms.

My heart was suddenly pounding faster than it should and my mouth dried up. "Um. Who are you?"

"Agent Katherine Price, but you can call me Kitty," she said with a wink. The wink broke me and the spell she had on me.

She was just a little too perfect and definitely not right. I felt a snap in my head and suddenly she didn't seem quite so perfect. I could see the too-thin frame and acne scars. Her too pretty exterior was like a picture that had been put over top. I could see it if I focused, but if not, it was a ghostly transparent image.

Like everyone else, she glowed with a faint aura. Unlike everyone else, hers was purple. She was the only person other than my mom, Eve, and Dean that hadn't been blue or green. I wondered what that meant.

Her image was fake, but the badge was real and it said Elmsley Science Corps.

"I don't know who or what you are, but last I heard from Harold, he was going to the old mine to investigate the green goo. Now go the hell away."

CHAPTER 8

I insisted on working my shift that night. Eve and Mom tried to convince me I wasn't up to it, but Eve had to help her aunt and Mom was bringing a special delivery to the café in Nushka. She always wanted to bring it herself. I think she has a crush on the owner.

"Are you sure you're going to be okay?"

"Mom, for the billionth time, yes. I'm literally steps away from home, and Jordan is just in the kitchen with all the sharp knives." I pointed at the door. She nodded and headed out.

Poking his dishevelled blond head out from the kitchen, Jordan asked, "What happened to make her all protective?" His heavy French from France accent, as opposed to Canadian French, made him sound judgemental to my ears, but I'd known him since I was in diapers and it just wasn't his way. He glowed a golden aura like Eve.

After I explained to him everything that had happened, he smirked and got a dangerous twinkle in his eye as he said, "Don't worry. I'll protect you." I tried not to laugh as he juggled his chef's knife. I had no doubt he was dangerous, but it was funny to see the smiling man who I'd passed in height at ten years old act tough.

"I doubt they'll come to the diner," I said and took a long drink of my coffee. The warm sweet liquid made me feel comforted and calm. I may have a problem, and I'm not sure if I care.

"I've seen some weird shit. Back in the eighties I was the chef at a summer camp that turned out to be a government lab. That was messed up." He said it like it wasn't a big deal and I wasn't sure he should. I mean, was I any different? There was some sort of green eyed thing taking over the senior class, and I wasn't freaking out or anything. *Should I be? I'm not sure.* The idea that Harold and that Katherine woman were looking into things should have made me feel like it was being taken care of. Instead, I was worried and trying not to care all at once.

My shift started out weird and only got worse. My first customers seemed to have picked their wardrobes off an FBI or MIB movie set. They were both in their mid-thirties, she was ridiculously beautiful with blonde hair and white skin, his nose had been broken enough times to make him rugged, but his hazel eyes were full on puppy. I could see tattoos peeking out of his shirt sleeves and collar, they were vivid black on his golden brown skin.

Both agents could have been retired underwear models or superheroes. She glowed blue, but it was tinged with emerald green, making her seem almost aqua. It was a stark contrast from the dull green of my classmates. He glowed a bright yellow, not the golden warmth of Eve and Jordan, but something brighter.

I took their order and asked, "Is there anything else I can get you?"

"We were wondering if you had seen anything strange the past year or so." The man had a distinctly Eastern Ontario accent.

"I've seen a lot of strange stuff. What are you looking for specifically?" My heart sped up. I'd watched too many movies since this summer. If Harold was a government official in a movie, he was the spunky young adult kind. These guys were more of the action or horror movie types.

"We've heard reports of weird animals and strange lights in the sky." She didn't phrase it like a question, but it was.

I laughed. "This is Northern Ontario. We have the second highest rate of reports for flying saucers and alien abductions. Hell, Moonbeam has a giant statue of a UFO. If you've heard stories, that's probably all they are." I'd done a report on aliens in Northern Ontario. There were more stories than I thought possible, but nothing was real. Then again, maybe the green goo was an alien thing despite what Harold had said?

"Nonetheless, we'd appreciate it if you keep your eyes and ears open." The woman reached into her suit jacket, and I could see the gun holster. These two were for real. She pulled out a simple white matte business card. It had a golden Y at the top, her name, and her phone number.

"Agent Kennedy Johnson," I read. "Who are you?" Since when did military people go around with business cards?

"We're part of Yggdrasil Command, a team that investigates these kinds of things." Her voice was deep and soft. That, her emerald green eyes, and the way she put her words together reminded me of Doctor Batudev.

"Okay." I left and gave Jordan the order.

"That took you a long time." His accent seemed thicker.

"They're investigating alien stuff."

"I have my citizenship papers!" He seemed nervous.

"Not that kind of alien." I pointed up and hummed the X-files theme.

"Oh, okay," he said, but that didn't seem to calm him down.

The diner was nice and full. Mondays always were. It's as if everyone who travelled for a living liked doing it on Monday. The great thing about it was they were all adults and all used to the road. No parents, no bratty children, and no entitled idiots. Just truckers, delivery people, and apparently sexy government types. I wondered if all government workers were that hot or if I just had the best luck. The group was much more diverse in auras than the rest of town. Lots of pink, yellow, gold, and blue.

When Fred came in, I was happy to see him. His aura matched the big government agent. He went over to the counter and sat down like his three hundred pounds weighed twice as much.

"What's with the long face, Fred?" I touched his hand as I poured his usual coffee.

"Reminds me about a joke about a horse." He chuckled. "The roads are really crowded. Something is going on. Way too many unmarked cars and that's not even mentioning the checkpoints."

When I came back with his order, he gestured at the two suits and said, "Those people are running checkpoints. Pretending to be MADD or OPP."

"They told me they were military." I showed him the card.

Swearing softly, he said, "That's what's going on? Freaking aliens?"

He sighed, his shoulders released tension as he relaxed and added, "Annoying, but not my problem." That was good to know, I was starting to expect monsters, aliens, and military everywhere, but maybe it wasn't my problem either. "I like the glasses. Very chic," he said, but he pronounced it like a baby chicken.

By the time the dinner rush ended around ten, things always slowed down. Fred was making jokes with Jordan, and the two military people had finished their meals. Sitting there with their food for over three hours was odd. It was like they were waiting for someone.

I started to clean and prepare for the next day. There were a dozen people in various states of eating when the large underwear model, I mean military guy, got up and went to the washroom.

There was a weird lull in conversation as he left. Like everyone was worried he was going toward them. The silence was broken by Sergeant Bannerman coming into the restaurant. His eyes reflected light like a cat's in the nighttime. I leaned against the counter to avoid falling, his entire body was blurry, everything but his eyes, and it was messing with my head.

He sat across from Agent Johnson and said loudly, "What are you doing here?" He leaned forward and his body language was definitely threatening.

"Sergeant?" She glanced at his rank on his uniform and handed him a card, "We're here looking for a few dangerous fugitives. Like I told your officer earlier, we'd appreciate your cooperation."

He actually growled at her, and said, "This town belongs to the One. The One doesn't want you or your partner. Leave town and if I see you again, I'll make sure you never find your fugitive."

Cocking an eyebrow, the woman said, "We'll be on our way once we're done with our meal."

"You seem done to me."

"We haven't had pie, and I love the coffee here. Can I buy you a cup?"

He hissed and exited the restaurant.

From behind me, the soft voice of the male military guy asked, "Something's wrong with him. Do you know what?"

"Yes," I replied, trying to get my heart out of my throat. He'd surprised me and I was having all kinds of awkward thoughts about him being this close. I guess my mind would rather go to horny than terrified. I don't blame it.

"Could you tell me?"

"You wouldn't believe me."

"Try me." His eyes sparkled with humour like I'd said something funny. This close, I could see scars on his arms and neck under his tattoos.

"There's a pool of green goo that seems to have infected the police and the high school seniors. I'm not sure what it is or what it wants, but their touch freezes and they call themselves the One. I'm fairly certain they hate me, but I'm not sure why." It all came tumbling out. I felt both foolish and relieved to tell someone. There was something calming about the giant man.

"Hm. We'll look into this. Where is the pool?"

I told him and asked him, "Is this alien?"

He nodded at his partner as she headed to the washroom.

Smiling, he responded, "No, but if no one else is here, we might as well see what we can do."

"There is someone else here, an Agent Price and Lieutenant Harnel from something called Elmsley."

His brow furrowed, obviously annoyed. He opened his mouth as if to speak, but before he could, he turned his head to the door, pulled out his gun, and shot some sort of energy blast at a woman who just walked in.

The violence of it caught everyone, except the woman, by surprise. We all just stood there for a moment as the government agent and the random woman started shooting at each other.

The momentary shock didn't last too long, and all of a sudden people were screaming and throwing themselves out of the way. I just ducked.

"You cannot stop us from finding her," said the woman in a choppy sort of accent. She was wearing a black one piece suit with a silver wave that went from her left ankle to her right breast. It was skin tight and extremely attractive. Her hair was loose shoulder length, black with frosted blue tips.

"Earth is an independent planet. You have no authority here. Leave and no one gets hurt." The big agent spoke like he knew nothing would work but had to go through the motions anyway.

"Get the hell off my planet!" The female agent said as she came out of the washroom shooting and her blasts hit the new woman in the chest.

She fell to the ground and looked up at the agent, smirking, "We will get her, and your planet will burn." She reached into a pocket and threw a ball behind the counter where I was half hiding, half watching.

The ball beeped. "That's not good," I said and grabbed a metal pot and put it over the ball, which I was fairly certain was a grenade or bomb. Jordan ran out of the kitchen and put his hand over the pot.

"I'm sorry, but your mom would kill me if I didn't do this." He gave me a sad half-smile and his hands started to glow; it spread to the bowl and the beep accelerated. He started sweating and swore in French.

I put my hand on his shoulder, and he relaxed. I should have run, I should have been afraid, but I was just numb.

The bomb went off with a sound that was a little softer than the sigh we all released afterward.

I heard the hum of the agent's gun before I saw it. For the second time that night, I did something on instinct. I stood between Jordan and the military.

"Please, I'm just a cook. Nothing special." Jordan lifted his hands.

"Leave him alone," I said. My vision turned green, and I felt cold and angry.

The agent put away his gun and in an almost bored tone asked, "What are you?"

"Arinitian, but I was born in France." Jordan's voice quivered.

The quiver made me angrier than I had ever been before I said, "Get out! I don't care who you are, but get out." I took a step forward and both of them took a step backward.

Looking past me at Jordan, the big man said, "Thank you for saving everyone's lives."

"Jason, did you see any aliens tonight?" Kennedy asked, holstering her weapon.

"Yep. One assassin."

"Any others?"

"Nope." He smirked, winked at me, and roughly tossed the unconscious alien over his shoulder. As they left, he said, "Remember when they used to teleport away? I miss that." On their table was a wad of bills worth twice their meal.

I sat down next to the coffee maker and poured myself another cup. The warm liquid calmed me, and I glanced around.

"The place seems good," I said and sighed. I suddenly wished I'd paid attention to the alien women's aura. In the frantic action movie scene that had become my life, I'd just not noticed.

"A destroyed pot and scorch mark on the floor are pretty good considering a bomb and shootout." Jordan sounded shook up.

Putting my now empty cup down, I hugged him and said, "It's okay. I won't tell mom if you don't want me to, and there were no locals who saw anything."

"Your mom knows, and thank you."

"I do have to ask. Do you know what the assassin wanted?" I wasn't sure he would tell me even if he knew, but I was curious.

Sighing, he said, "There are rumours of a lost princess. I don't really know much but she's escaped some sort of war and is supposed to be hiding on Earth."

There was something about a lost alien princess that was both tragic, sexy, and silly to me. "Wow, talk about hunting in the wrong place."

He laughed nervously, and we went on with our regular business. When things slowed down I asked him about aliens in general. I guess he thought I was asking about his powers. "The story my mother told me was that a long time ago there was a great galactic war, and we used genetic engineering to give ourselves advantages. My people valued protecting each other, but others wanted weapons. It took my people almost a thousand years to recover. When they did, the galaxies were ruled by greedy empires and cults. My family escaped to Earth hoping no one would ever find us."

"You mean the universe is just teeming with aliens? Fighting and living and loving just like humans?" I felt very small and unimportant all of the sudden.

"No, not like humans. Earth is one of the most dangerous planets in the universe where life can still survive. A lot of aliens can't even eat your food. You drink literal poison for fun." He looked awed.

"You can't have alcohol? What about spicy food?" I asked.

Smiling he replied, "I'm okay. My people's alterations were about protecting ourselves. Healers too, but most aliens have to be really careful. There are only a dozen species in the known universe that can tolerate theobromine. You eat it in bulk for fun. It would literally explode most living things' hearts. Your people are scary." Theobromine was one of the components of chocolate. My favourite kind was from a little chocolate shop called Chocolate Death in Shields Crossing, Ontario that used my mom's coffee inside it.

"I get it. I get it," I said, raising my hands in surrender. It was weird to be proud of my species when I hated so many of them. He told me stories about his mother's homeworld, but he was very vague on details. More like fairytales than documentaries.

Only a few truckers came in after that, and then we closed. Fred stuck around and as we got ready to lock up, he asked, "You want me to walk you to your door?"

It sounded silly, I lived on top of the restaurant, my door was less than ten metres, but I wasn't comfortable going alone after tonight, or after the past week for that matter. "That would be great."

As we got to the door, I turned and kissed Fred on the cheek, "Thank you. You didn't have to stick around after all—" I waved my hands. "You must be far behind schedule for your route."

"Don't worry about it. I'd hate myself for leaving."

I watched him leave, and then locked the door. Mom wasn't supposed to be home until tomorrow so I had the house to myself. Normally that would have excited me, and I would have turned up some music, watched a movie, or viewed some naughty websites, but I wasn't in the mood for any of that.

When I closed my eyes, I saw the sergeant and Richard. That shift had been overly stressful, and I felt like I was losing a battle with sanity. I felt so tired.

I made a pot of coffee and grabbed my laptop. From the couch, I logged into social media and checked my friends. Most of the town had unfriended me or blocked me when they thought I was a murderer, so it was mostly people I know from competitions, family, and random people who'd added me.

I was hoping that Eve would be online. This had been a terrible day, and yet, the thought of our terribly messed up date made me smile.

"So did you do it?" Bart asked. I had to scroll up in our conversation to remember what we'd talked about.

I smirked at myself and replied, "Are you asking if I masturbated?"

"I hate you, cuz." He put a blush emoji. When I didn't reply, he continued, "No! Did you tell either of your crushes how you feel?"

"Oh, I told one of them. The other seems to have disappeared."

"So...?" He seemed eager in a way that would be comical if I could see it.

"I went on a date. It was wonderful. Until the end."

"Did something happen?" He was probably expecting me to say something like she wasn't into me or didn't realize it was a date.

"Can we video chat?" I asked. I didn't want a text trail of everything I was going to tell him.

The feed was good, and I could see him and hear him clearly. It was a sign of how much everything had changed in the past year. Last year I'd have used the video chat as an excuse to stop chatting with my dance friends and flirting with Veronica and listen to Bart's drama. I suddenly felt very alone and isolated.

"I'm sorry I didn't believe you, cuz."

His face didn't change much, but he did smirk as he feigned innocence. Sarcastically, he said, "You didn't believe me that my girlfriend, who'd been missing, had been turned into a mitten by an evil wizard who was taken down by a scrappy ninth grader? Or did you not believe me that a genie was granting wishes and screwing with reality? Oh wait, it must have been the story of how that same scrappy ninth grader went back in time and ended up being my Dad's first kiss?"

"You left out your summer camp time loop." I paused and put on my best deadpan bitchy voice and added, "Actually it was the part where you had a girlfriend." We both laughed. The jokes hid the pain we both felt and the frustrations we had with our respective situations.

"So why are you suddenly so willing to believe my ridiculous life?" he asked, and I could see little lines of worry crinkling his eyes and forehead. He acted tough and like nothing bothered him, but he was a big softy and cared more than I deserved.

"Because my life has gotten really weird in the past few weeks."

"Go ahead. Let me have it. Nothing surprises me anymore."

I started by telling him again what had happened that summer, sparing no details. I told him everything that happened and everything I was worried about.

When I was done, I paused and he asked, "Aliens? Like from…" he trailed off and pointed up toward the sky. I nodded and he said, "Well shit, Hel. I'm glad I didn't bet you on my being surprised. Do you need help? Have you talked to your mom?"

"I have sort of talked to Mom, but I need to get everything from her when she gets back, and I don't know if I need help. I have Eve, Mom, and more government agents than I know what to do with. I think I'm okay."

That's when the power went out, and with it, the internet. I checked my phone, and it said no signal.

CHAPTER 9

Playing sad violin music in the dark was creepy. Somehow when I switched to a jig it wasn't any better. I'm not sure when I fell asleep, but I did and my dreams were filled with green sludge. The last one I remembered, I was watching Harold get eaten by the same pool as Richard.

I woke up with someone shaking me. In my terror, I reached out and pushed them away. A crash and a pained moan brought me fully awake.

I'd thrown Eve across the room and against my mom's bedroom door. I got up as quickly as I could, my phone and empty coffee cup falling to the ground. The blanket I was wrapped in tried to trip me but I managed to only stumble.

"Are you okay?" I asked part numb, part terrified as I bent over to touch her cheek.

She laughed. It was a pained laugh, but still a laugh. Her whole face lit up with joy and it made me feel warm and loved. It was the same warmth I felt when my mom gave me a loving smile, but it was different too, different in a way that made me warm in my core.

As I helped Eve up, she said, "You're stronger than I expected. Good thing I'm tough."

"Did you break anything?"

"Your mom's door, I think."

I fought a snort of laughter and said, "Stand still. I want to make sure." I gently ran my hands over her back, arms, and legs. It was a check I'd done a million times with other dancers. It was meant to be clinical, but when it came to Eve, I had trouble not thinking about her soft curves and pleasingly muscled back. A soft moan escaped her mouth, and I wanted nothing more than to kiss her and find out what other sounds she could make.

Instead, I fell to the ground gripping my head. My pain was green and I swear I heard Harold screaming. My phone rang at the same time. I stumbled over and picked it up.

"Miss Benson? This is Agent Price from yesterday. You said my partner had gone to an old mine, but there are a dozen mines around here and he's not answering his phone." She stopped there. Her voice was collected, but I'd done enough dance competitions to recognize someone faking calm.

"It's the one at the end of Highway 2. Just go past the diner and take a— you know what. No. Meet me in the diner in twenty minutes."

Eve's face showed both confusion and curiosity.

"I need a shower and then I'm treating you to breakfast. But first I need to make a call." I picked up my phone and went to my room. I searched yesterday's uniform and found the card for the military alien people.

I dialled the number and a female voice answered, "Go for Kennedy." I was expecting military brusqueness, not peppy.

"Um. Agent Johnson?"

"Yes. How can I help you, Helen?" She must have caller ID.

"Remember we talked about a pool of sludge? I think it's eaten a guy from another military group, and his partner wants to go check on him. Can you meet us at the diner in twenty minutes?"

"Sure. We need some breakfast anyway." She hung up.

Eve gave me a funny look and I said, "Long story, but I'm going to get the military and the military to get together and go save Harold."

"Great, 'cause we have class in fifty minutes."

"Shit," was my only response, and I rushed for the shower. I tried to think of pleasant things in the shower without getting too distracted, but I was feeling weak and dizzy by the time I got out. I stared in my closet and sighed. I didn't put as much effort into my outfits as I had before this summer, but right now, I wanted quick and simple. I grabbed my favourite orange sweater dress. It had a cowl neck and hugged me in a way that always made me feel warm and a little sexy. I grabbed a pair of black leggings to go with it. My backpack had some makeup and a hair tie in it.

The Yggdrasil agents arrived first. I'd just finished my first cup of coffee, did some quick makeup, and was sitting while Eve braided my hair.

The blonde agent saw Eve and pursed her lips like she was trying really hard not to say anything.

"Do you two know each other?" I asked.

"I've known Kennedy and Jason since I was a kid. Before I moved to Vancouver Island I lived in Westmeath." Both the agents were visibly relieved and rushed her for a hug. The three hugged, and I saw tears in Kennedy's eyes.

"Are you okay? How are you holding up?" the blonde woman asked.

"I'm good," Eve replied and smiled at me. I felt my insides quiver a little.

"I'm glad," Kennedy said but before she could say anything else, the redhead walked into the diner. Kennedy and Eve separated and went back to acting like they didn't know each other.

The three agents sat down, and grumped in each other's directions.

"Agents Johnson, this is Agent Price."

It was Kennedy who spoke first, "Yggdrasil Command, and you're with?"

"Elmsley, Science Division," the redhead said. Eve had gone back to doing my hair and paused a little when she heard the name.

"Is this goo your jurisdiction or ours?" the larger agent asked.

"My partner was convinced it was ours, but I honestly have no clue." She sounded tired and scared.

"Would you like some unofficial help? We owe the young Miss Benson for last night."

"As long as it's unofficial." She hesitated a little.

By this point I'd had two coffees and had finally warmed up. My mind was clear and I was feeling rather well for someone who fell asleep sitting up. "You're not here officially are you?" I asked. When she shook her head, I added, "Why are you here?"

She sighed a little too dramatically, and said, "Harold heard about what happened this summer and wanted to investigate. Our bosses denied us, and he took some vacation. When he didn't answer my calls, I came looking for him."

Her voice was snippy and defensive. *Wasn't I supposed to be the teenager here?*

"Wow. Well okay then. Thanks for all that. Now you three can take care of it and I'll head to class. Bye!" I'd already texted them the directions to the mine. I felt that at least the Yggdrasil agents were competent.

I hoped they would at least save Harold and best case, stop the green goo. Although I couldn't imagine what they'd do for that.

On the ride to school, I sent a quick text to Bart telling him I was okay. He replied immediately which showed he was worried.

The rest of the day was completely uneventful. I got glares from the normal people and the green eyed ones. Eve was quiet most of the day and barely said anything until we headed back home.

Finally, I asked, "Do you trust the Johnsons?"

"Yes. Without a doubt," she answered. Her usual sing-song almost spacey tone was replaced with complete conviction. "How did you meet them?"

"I met them during my shift last night."

"Do you know why they're here?" Her eyes were on the road, but I could tell she was paying a lot of attention to what I was saying.

Making a split second gut instinct decision is what got me ostracized and accused of murder. That's what I'd been telling myself all summer and fall, but it was bullshit. Had I been the perfect little bisexual and never cheated but had an honest relationship, the town would still have treated me like I was some sort of monster.

"Aliens," I said and when she didn't react, I explained everything that happened, leaving out Jordan. I'd be a terrible person if I outed him, even if I personally trusted Eve.

When I was done explaining, I expected her to be surprised or to laugh it off. Instead, she was worried and a little pale. I wasn't sure what to say or do, so I did nothing.

"Do you want to stay for dinner?" I asked when we pulled into the diner.

"Are you working?"

"Not tonight. Tomorrow and Thursday."

Eve's eyes focused at a distance and she gave a giant sigh. "Aliens. What do you think about that?"

"Seems more realistic than the other stuff happening. Plus, a runaway alien princess? *Hot!*"

She giggled and said, "You *would* say that. But seriously, it doesn't freak you out?"

"In the past five months, I've been accused of murder, been unable to sleep without nightmares, and been shunned for being bisexual. In the past two weeks, my ex has turned into some sort of goo monster with the rest of the senior class, I've been attacked by police and had gunk puked into my eyes, met people with special abilities, and found out my mom knew about all of it. No, I'm not freaked out by aliens. I've hit peak freaked out, and I just can't deal anymore."

Putting her hand on mine, Eve bent over and kissed me. Her lips were soft, wet, and warm. I'd had a lot of experience kissing before, but when she kissed me, my whole body tingled, and every part of me vibrated with pleasure. I had thought I was horny before, but that kiss dialled it up to eleven.

"Plus, the aliens seem to be people, not monsters bent on destroying the world, so I'm cool with that," I added breathlessly after the kiss.

"You wouldn't be scared if you found out someone you knew was an alien?" She sounded flustered, and I'm fairly certain it was the kiss.

"No." I was thinking of Jordan and how little it bothered me.

I kissed her several more times on the way up to the apartment. Mom should have been home, and I didn't want to make out in front of her.

I unlocked the door and no one was home. She should have been home that morning. I sent her a text and started preparing supper. Mom had some frozen rainbow trout from a local fisherman, and I defrosted one large fillet. I prepared it with some fresh jalapenos and pineapple. I also made some roasted vegetables and some wild rice to go with it.

Eve watched and helped as I cooked. I'm not sure if it was the kiss, the hope that the military would take care of my troubles, or that I love cooking, but I found myself dancing through the kitchen.

When the meal was ready and my mom still hadn't replied, I called down to the restaurant. One of the other servers answered and passed me to Jordan. His thick accent was harder to understand on the phone. "Your mother sent me an email telling me she'd be a few days longer and that I should carry on without her."

"Was she on the schedule for this week?"

"No, it was a roasting week for her. I'll have to fix next week though. Are you available for extra shifts?" Once a month, my mother would hide away in the roastery and make amazing amounts of roasted beans. She always did it alone and always came out starving and really tired.

"Sure."

We ate dinner in complete silence. I was fighting with too many emotions and a headache. At the end of the meal, Eve smiled and told me how amazing it was. We cleaned the kitchen together and playfully teased each other.

I made coffee and the two of us stood awkwardly with no more social rituals to keep us from thinking sexy thoughts. Her beautiful full cheeks turned red as I ogled her and I asked, "Do you want to stay a little? We could watch a movie."

"Why don't we jam?" she asked.

My brain tried as hard as it could to think of a sexy meaning for the word and couldn't. After staring blankly at her, I said, "We just ate."

Her face fell and she said, "I just thought, I brought my flute."

I felt like a complete fool and laughed. "Oh, music. I'm sorry, my head is pounding and I didn't understand. Please let's play." I drank some coffee, and my headache receded.

Her flute was made of light ash wood, was straight like a recorder and large. There were dark etchings all around the body.

"That's beautiful. What key is it? Is that a bass, so F?" I blurted out quickly.

"Yes. It is. I'm quite proud of it." She put it to her lips and my insides trembled, both from the gorgeous sound, and my desire to be the flute pressed up against her lips.

I picked up my violin and together we played a few classical pieces and then tried to improvise. It devolved into a horny orchestra sound, and we both burst out laughing.

"Movie?" she asked. I nodded, with no intention of watching the movie.

We actually did put on a movie. I'm not sure what it was, but it played while we kissed. I wanted to touch, kiss, and lick every part of her. I wanted to explore her body so much it ached, but I also didn't want to go too quickly.

We kissed and touched and forgot about everything else for an evening, but unfortunately, it had to end. Eve had to go back to her aunt's, and I stayed up finding my own release.

Wednesday started as an average day, and I was lulled into a sense of normalcy. The seniors were still all green eyed and evil, but they seemed to be avoiding me. It's amazing what kind of stuff you can get used to.

One thing I was not getting used to was holding Eve's hand and stealing kisses. Unfortunately, we weren't in all the same classes.

As I headed to biochem, I was daydreaming about Eve's curves, when I heard the familiar sound of a dying lizard.

"Helen. I've been meaning to speak to you." Miss Lacroix was wearing a black sweater and white pants. The black with her black hair and pale skin gave me the, unfortunately wrong, impression of a hot goth chick.

"I'm on my way to class."

"Yes, I know, but Mister Smith asked me to talk with you. Come see me after school in my office."

Biochem was Dean-less and quiet. It was nice to lose myself in taking notes.

Outside the door, Steve was waiting for me. "Hel, still an abomination against God?"

"Steve, still an abomination against good taste?" I responded by instinct, but then froze. He was fondling his crucifix like it would give him an orgasm. More importantly his eyes were a dull brown, and he wasn't fuzzy at all. He actually glowed a light blue like he was a normal person.

"If you don't stop making a spectacle of your lifestyle, some of us might have to teach you a lesson."

He was threatening me and I should be shocked, horrified, or angry, but instead I was overjoyed. Fighting the urge to hug him, I said, "My lifestyle is fine for you when you're alone with your phone in the bathroom." When his eyes grew big and angry, I added, "Glad to have you back, you homophobic bigot."

I turned away and heard him hit a locker. I didn't care. If Steve was back to his old horrific self that meant the nice military folks had done their job, and I was goo free. I was so excited I skipped through the halls like a cartoon schoolgirl.

My day was great. I was still being insulted and judged, but no creepy things happened, just normal human monsters.

Eve offered to come with me to my meeting with Miss Lacroix, but I told her not to worry. Things were going back to 'survive high school and get out' instead of 'don't get goo-i-fied'. She decided to go to the library and wait for me.

Miss Lacroix's office smelled of paint, clay, and incense. I was surprised she was allowed to burn that stuff in school.

"Helen. Glad you made it." Her wide mouth formed a practised benign smile. It was the smile that politicians and priests use when they want to put someone at ease.

"You didn't give me much choice, Miss Lacroix," I said, matching her sugary tone. If she wanted to be all fake pleasant, I was willing to play along.

"I'm sorry about that, but I've watched you go down a dark path these past few months. You're not the same vibrant girl I remember from my senior year." She paused, probably to let me argue, but I just kept my fake smile and raised my eyebrow, doing my best imitation of Spock. When I didn't say anything, she continued, "Why did you quit dance?"

"I was accused of murdering my classmate's brother and the rest of the studio rallied against me. I didn't feel much like going after that."

"Hm. What led to the murder accusation?" she asked. I was starting to see where she was going, but I decided to play innocent.

"At a party one night, my boyfriend fell into a rage, and then into a pit of green goo. He disappeared, and I was accused of his murder until he came back."

Waving dismissively as if my answer were a pesky fly, she said, "Yes, yes. But what led to that event?"

"My boyfriend's sister hit on me, and I lacked the emotional intelligence to say no." She wanted the truth.

"Interesting. That's not the story I heard. Veronica says that it was you who assaulted her." She reached for a cup that was in front of her. There were two cups with brownish liquid broth. She stopped and reached for the other, bringing it up to her lips to drink.

I smirked. Probably a little too much because she started to squirm before I started to speak, "So she didn't tell you about our first kiss?" I didn't wait for her to answer before continuing, "I was over at their house for dinner and after we'd all finished eating, Richard and I went downstairs to 'watch' a movie. It was mostly making out. He's a competent kisser, but he knows exactly where to put his hands. After an hour or so, I needed a break or I might lose my self-control. Richard had been pressuring me to have sex for over a year.

"I went to the washroom to calm myself down, and I didn't think to lock the door. Veronica came in as I was splashing cold water on my face. She was wearing short shorts and a crop-top with no bra. She told me she'd been watching us make out, and it had turned her on. She rubbed herself up against me and—" I stopped to get my thoughts together. It was a really sexy memory despite being a terrible decision. Miss Lacroix was crimson, but didn't stop me from continuing. "Her soft lips tasted of vanilla and orange, and every part of her was dancer's muscles. We kissed and my hands wandered. I was weak and shouldn't have given in."

"Jesus," she said with pure embarrassment and disgust. "Have you spoken to your religious leader about your unhealthy urges?"

I guess the old stereotype of homophobes being repressed gay wasn't always right.

"I just need a rabbi and an imam to complete the set."

Chapter 10

She seemed confused at the comment, but quickly fell back into her smile. Taking a deep calming breath, she said, "I understand that the world is a confusing place at your age. Hormones are going wild, movies and television are plastered with sin." I scoffed; she was three years older than me, not thirty. "But I have found great solace in accepting Jesus and God into my heart."

"Congratulations." My snark was calculated. She was way out of line for a public school.

"I understand how you feel. You think all this anger is part of you and that it protects you. You need to learn to accept faith and know it'll make you stronger. Jesus is a guide to your salvation, not a tyrant to control your life." Again she reached for the first of two cups, stopped herself and drank from the other.

I stood up and said, "You know what? I was having a great day before this. You want to talk about my sexuality and sex life? Fine, let's talk. I am sexually attracted to people: men, women, and if I met someone who was neither or both, I'm sure I could be attracted to them, too."

"That's a dangerous lifestyle." She stood up and furrowed her brow in worry.

I sighed, what was the point of talking with her about this? She didn't care about anything but her own biases. "Believe what you want, Miss Lacroix, but leave me out of it." I turned and started to leave.

"Miss Benson, we are having a discussion." She sounded angry.

I felt defeated in a way and just wanted to leave. I tried for bitchy, but only managed disinterested. "A discussion I don't want to have, with a teacher who I'm not taking any classes with, on a subject that is none of your business."

The door opened, and Richard, Steve, and Veronica walked in. Richard was smug, but at least Veronica had the decency to be uncomfortable.

As if this was planned, Miss Lacroix continued. "As I was saying, a few students approached me about your lifestyle."

The three of them blocked the exit. My heart started pounding, and I started feeling panicked. What were they going to do to me?

I was in full panic when I noticed their eyes. They were natural colours and my vision wasn't all weird around them, just like earlier with Steve. This was high school bullying, not a monster attack. I mentally chastised myself for panicking.

Targeting Veronica, I said, "Let me get this straight, you were upset I was with your brother not you, then you were upset I was with you, now you're upset I found someone else? Seriously, get some help."

"I'm not a lesbian. You just tricked me, and I'm worried about your soul." She wasn't going to win any acting awards. At that moment I was angry, angry about people being shitty, angry about this situation, and angry in general.

I wasn't angry at her, I was angry *for* her. I had accepting parents and despite this damned town, I was going to be okay. She had no one to support her. Hopefully she'd go away to college or university and be able to find some sort of peace inside herself.

I turned to Miss Lacroix. "Life is about balance and acceptance. If your Jesus encourages hate, fear, and whatever the hell this is." I gestured around wildly. "Then you should probably try to find a better religion. Leave me alone, or I will complain to the school board, the teacher's union, and anyone else who will listen. It might be the 1950s in this school and town, but the rest of the world is in 2015."

I'd had enough and moved to push myself through the three blocking the door. I took one step, and my head exploded in pain. Everything turned green, then black. I fell to my knees and waited for the pain to lessen. It didn't, but I started to get used to it and was able to open my eyes.

I hadn't noticed Miss Lacroix moving around her desk, but I could feel her warm hand on my shoulder. Before my eyes, Veronica's posture changed from awkward and uncomfortable to confident. Her eyes glowed green and the rest of her became distorted.

"The One is eternal and will never stop. You will be part of the One." All three of them said the same thing, but they were slightly out of sync.

"What's going on?" Miss Lacroix's hand tightened on my shoulder, and she stood up.

"This one has fought the One too long. We will bring her to the well, and she shall become One."

As indignantly as possible, Miss Lacroix said, "I asked you three to help me, not pull some juvenile prank. Get out of my office!"

She'd ambushed me with her twisted morals and made me feel like I should be ashamed of who I love, but in that moment she stood up for me. Her protective instincts took over. I have to give her credit for that.

Richard backhanded her so hard she cleared the desk and landed against a pile of painted student canvases.

The pain in my head evened out, and I realized I'd been feeling it since this summer. I didn't know what it meant, but I had more important things to think about at that moment.

I got up and backed up. The office had a back door that led to the art room. If I could make it there, I had a chance of getting to the outside door in the classroom.

By the time I stood up and started moving, Veronica was blocking my exit.

Backing up, I bumped into Miss Lacroix who was now standing behind the desk. "What's wrong with them?" she whimpered.

"Some sort of green goo parasite thing."

"Okay," she replied, a mixture of terror and disbelief in her tone.

The three of them were in front of me now, the desk behind me in the small office.

I didn't know what to do. I grabbed the two cups on Miss Lacroix's desk and tossed their contents at the goo zombies. Whatever was in them hit Richard and Steve in the face and caused them to be thrown back. They knocked over a plant near the door and pulled a few art posters off the wall. They recoiled in pain and horror into the hallway, while Veronica screamed even though nothing had hit her.

Both of us ran for the door. I was a little bit faster and made it out when I heard a scream. Veronica had Miss Lacroix. She had a hand on each of the older woman's ears, both leaning over with the desk between them, and for a second I thought she was going in for a kiss.

Miss Lacroix's screams were cut short by a stream of green goo that shot from Veronica's mouth into hers.

I gagged a little and ran. At first I was just running, but then I remembered that Eve was in the library. I needed to warn her. Thankfully, it seemed that most people, goo people included, had gone home. I ran through the empty halls, my heart beat and footsteps the only sound other than my breathing.

When I got to the library, I almost ran into Amanda, Lindsay, and Lacey. They were all banging on the library doors. The glass double doors were barricaded from the inside, but they wouldn't hold.

I did my best to quietly stop and failed miserably as my shoes squeaked on the floor. The three girls, slightly fuzzy, turned in unison and stared at me.

I swore loudly and backed up, into the arms of Veronica. "Funny, I thought we were done," I said meekly as Veronica held me in a bear hug.

Amanda stepped forward and opened her mouth. I closed mine, but Lacey grabbed my nose and Lindsay my jaw. I'd had a dream like this once, but it had involved more nakedness and less mind control.

Just as I thought I was about to swallow a lot of goo, Amanda fell to the ground. Dean stood behind her with a library chair. The other three screeched, but he smacked Lacey with the chair and Eve ran out of the library and hit Lindsay. I stomped on Veronica's foot and whipped my head back to hit her in the nose. She let go. Blood started flowing from her nose. It started a dark red and changed into a green colour.

"Let's get out of here," Dean screamed.

The three of us started running toward the exit, and we made it to the cool night air of the parking lot before hearing footsteps behind us. Richard, Steve, Veronica, and the three girls were running after us. Eve unlocked the car and jumped in. Dean climbed into the back and I got in the front.

As we drove away, I saw that Richard and Steve's faces were discoloured like they had been burned. I pulled out my cell phone but had no reception.

"I don't have reception. Do any of you?" Dean shook his head, and Eve just handed me her phone. The whole network must have been down. I turned on the radio and could only get CBC. There was a tower nearby. Normally I'd get Timmins radio stations. "Something weird is going on."

"Can you drop me off at home? I have to check on my sister."

The streets were quiet as we drove to Elm Street and dropped Dean off. He muttered a *thanks* and *take care*, and then rushed out to the house. Eve waited until he'd gone in before driving off.

"What happened?" Eve must have been holding in that question for the entire ride.

"I don't know. Everything was normal and then..." I trailed off. When she didn't say anything, I told her all the details about the meeting.

"What do you think was in that cup?" she asked.

"I don't know. Paint? Maybe she had turpentine in it to clean brushes?" I had no idea.

As we pulled up to the diner, I sighed and Eve asked, "What's wrong? Other than the obvious which is enough to make you sigh, but I meant that sigh felt like it wasn't about the green goo-people."

"I have a shift, and you have to go check on your aunt." I put my hand on hers and leaned in to kiss her. I had meant for a quick peck, but it lasted longer and went deeper than I'd expected.

When we pulled away, she said, "I really should go."

"Yes, you should, before I rip your clothes off and carry you upstairs."

She giggled and promised to come back after she'd checked on her aunt.

I watched her leave and an ache in my chest told me I might never see her again. It was stronger than the pain in my head, but not by much.

In the diner, things seemed normal. The early dinner crowd was eating, and the atmosphere felt jovial. I made myself a coffee and went back to the kitchen to talk to Jordan. Every sip I took made me feel a little better.

"You're early," he said, smiling as he sautéed some onions.

"Do you have cell reception?" I asked. He checked his phone and shook his head. I went over to the office and tried the land line, but there was no dial tone. "Nothing in there either."

"Funny, we lost reception on all channels but CBC and Radio Canada on the radio," he said.

Just as I was finishing my coffee, one of the other servers came into the kitchen, "The debit isn't working."

Out front an elderly couple was waiting to pay their bill. I fiddled with the machine, but it seemed the internet and phone were down completely.

"We don't have cash," the man said indignantly.

Jordan came out with a block of metal and plopped it down on the table. With a proud smile, he pulled a stack of little papers out of his pocket and put them under the cash. "Let's do this old-school."

The machine had carbon paper and when you put a credit card under the paper and pulled the lever it imprinted the card details. You could then write the bill amount and have the client sign. He showed me and the server how to work it and what piece of paper to keep and what to give to the client.

The normalcy and problem solving of work calmed me down, and I felt almost human. I ran up the stairs, changed and headed back to work.

The tone in the diner had changed from casual and everyday to worry. People talked in hushed tones and ate quickly.

I spent the night expecting something terrible to happen, but nothing did. It felt like we were all waiting for a storm that was never going to come.

Near the end of my shift, Eve arrived seeming extra puzzled. She gave me a large phone-like thing and said, "It's an old walky-talky. I should be able to talk to you from across town."

She managed to say it in a sing-song voice that was both beautiful and a little creepy. Having her so close made my heart jump and skip for joy as I asked, "How's your aunt?"

"Totally normal. I expected, after the school and the near empty town, that she might be in trouble, but she was just in her office editing some stories. Congrats by the way."

"On what?"

She smirked and I wanted to rip all her clothes off right there inside the near empty diner. "You won the pumpkin carving contest. Although I think Allison did a great job, yours was really scary."

I had forgotten about the contest. It felt like years ago. "I bet Bob rigged it." I paused and said, "Copper Tarnish. What is that?"

Eve said, "As copper oxidizes it turns dark brown and then green. It's what gives parliament their distinctive green roofs. Why?"

"She said her pumpkin depicted the 'Copper Tarnish' folk story. And I've been seeing weird auras. Those who are goo-ed are green like oxidized copper."

She helped me clean up as I explained everyone's auras. She seemed especially surprised by her own golden hue.

As we were leaving, she asked, "What colour are you?"

I stopped as I was locking the doors and replied, "I have no idea. I haven't noticed anything in the mirror or if I stare at my hands."

She escorted me to my door, and I asked hopefully, "Want to come in?"

"I want to, but we both have an early morning tomorrow." She was talking about my MRI the next day. "I should go home. We can't all survive on no sleep with coffee and attitude," she teased.

"Don't forget spite and hormones," I added.

She kissed me goodbye and despite the fact that we seemed to be in the early parts of a zombie apocalypse and we had no contact with the outside world, she left me at my doorstep with nothing but a long-range walkie-talkie and a tingling on my lips.

I locked the door, braced a chair against it and tried to not think about how strong the goo-people were.

I took a quick shower, enjoying the heat, and examined myself in the mirror. I was blurry. I put on my glasses and I was the same as I remembered. I had bags under my grey eyes and I was obviously tired, but I couldn't see an aura on myself. I tried scanning my body and I could find any. Maybe I wasn't able to see mine or maybe I didn't have one?

I was just adding some sugar to my coffee when a crackling noise broke the silence startling me into a scream. I swore as I spilled some of the coffee onto my hand.

"H, this is E. Are you there? Over." Eve's voice came over the walkie-talkie, and I relaxed a little.

I pressed the talk button and in my best western accent said, "Roger, little lady. This is H." In my normal voice I added, "Why are we using code names? Over."

"It's safer in case someone can tap into the same frequency. Over."

"How about I'm Dancing Queen and you're Angeleyes? Over."

I heard laughter in her voice as she responded, "Alright Dancing Queen. I just wanted to make sure these work and that you're okay. Get some sleep, and I'll see you in the morning. Over."

"I'll try. Goodnight Angeleyes. I'll leave this thing on in case you need me. Over and out."

I would have rather talked with her all night or held her. Despite the hot coffee and blanket, I still felt cold. I turned up the heat and sat down to do some homework. I was behind on some assignments due. Being almost killed on a daily basis had that effect.

When the homework got blurry, I made another coffee and washed my glasses. It surprised me how fast I'd gotten used to them. Cleaning them did nothing for the blurriness, but the coffee helped a little.

I turned on the television and found nothing but static except on CBC. They were repeating the news.

"Our leading story is the chemical spill just north of Ansonville in Northern Ontario. RCMP are urging people to stay in their homes. Crews are cleaning up the spill that resulted from an overturned rail car." The rest of the coverage was from experts that didn't know anything.

I turned off the news and put in a movie. Before this, my go to comfort movie was *Resident Evil*, but that was a little too on the nose. I considered *Save the Last Dance* and shook my head. Dancing movies only made me feel sad now. I finally settled on *Princess Bride*.

I fell asleep in the fire swamp and my dreams were filled with Harold and Richard. They were laughing at the three government agents who were handcuffed together and covered in green goo. The strange thing was that Harold wasn't green like Richard.

The Elmsley agent, who'd introduced herself as Katherine, turned to me in my dream and said, "Help!"

CHAPTER 11

Have you ever been woken up by the smell of coffee and pancakes? Isn't it a wonderful smell to wake up to? Burnt coffee and pancakes when you're supposed to be alone and barricaded the door the night before is not as wonderful.

I jumped out of bed, grabbed the baseball bat I had taken out of the storage and slowly sneaked into the kitchen.

"Eve, what are you doing?" I relaxed once she turned around and I could see her eyes were blue.

"I got pancakes and coffee from the diner and put them in the oven to keep warm but couldn't remember how hot, and I think I pressed broil instead of bake." She was obviously frazzled as she collapsed onto one of the dining table chairs.

I turned off the oven and filled the sink with cold water before I found some metal tongs and fished what was left of the pancakes and the takeout container from the oven. The paper takeout cup had collapsed and there was a puddle inside the stove.

"Why don't we just go eat in the diner after I clean up?" I suggested.

She nodded and I could see the bags around her eyes. She pouted a little and I wanted nothing more than to kiss those lips. "I wanted to surprise you."

I laughed and said, "You did that for sure. How'd you get in? I braced the door with a chair and it was locked."

"Your mom gave me a key. When I pushed the door open, the chair fell." She shrugged. I should have known better than to just use the chair, it must have slipped.

The world flashed green and cold. I fell to the ground. Eve was next to me faster than I would have thought possible. She put a hand on my shoulder, and I saw her glow brighter. Suddenly, the green was gone, along with the headache I'd forgotten I had.

"You have magic hands," I said, trying to sound suggestive, but only managing tired.

Eve asked nervously, "Are you okay?"

I sat up and said, "Nothing some fresh coffee and food won't fix." I was putting on a brave face, and we both knew it.

I got dressed in a comfy pair of jeans and a loose sweater. I wasn't sure what the test would need, but I wanted to be comfortable if I needed to strip.

Breakfast was heavenly. I ate a lot more than I should have been able to, but I felt like it was a competition day. All wild energy, nerves, and hunger. Except that I only ate like this *after* a competition. It wasn't a diet thing, but if you're too full, it's harder to focus and you feel sluggish. Not good for competition. Not to mention nerves don't like things in my stomach.

I was starting to get used to seeing the world framed by my glasses. At least I was seeing the world. I noticed the military vehicles before I understood what they were.

When we got close enough, a uniformed man came to the driver window and when Eve rolled it down, he said, "Sorry kids, but no one gets in or out here."

I leaned over and showed him my doctor's referral and said, "I have a test in Timmins. I really don't want to miss it."

"Nothing I can do. Please head back." He had mastered being disinterested, but I could see him glancing at my and Eve's eyes. He knew something was going on.

We drove away and Eve said, "I guess we go to school."

"No. I doubt they know every back road out. I bet they don't know about the road through the Lacombe farm." I directed Eve through the back roads, some that could barely be considered paths. Thankfully it hadn't rained or snowed a lot, or we'd have gotten stuck in the mud.

It took twice as long, but we made it onto Highway 17 and somehow made it to my appointment only ten minutes late.

"Hello Miss Benson. I'm Doctor Shawn. Have you had an MRI before?" The doctor seemed nice. He explained that I had to take off all my jewellery and lie very still. He also did a few simple tests for my reflexes, eyesight, and cognitive abilities.

After the MRI, the doctor brought me and Eve into an office. "It'll take a day or two for us to send the information to your doctor, but from what I can see, your scans are completely normal.

"What about my headaches and vision issues?" I asked tentatively. He turned his head toward me, but seemed to be seeing past me like he was bored.

"Whatever you got in your eyes did damage, but there's nothing to indicate that it's affected any other part of you." He paused and added, "You really should be more careful with chemicals."

I bit back a snarky reply and instead asked, "And the headaches?"

"It's not uncommon for people who've had stressful events to start getting headaches. In my opinion," he gave Eve a pointed look, "I'd also recommend getting tested for STIs. Or it could just be your period."

I'm not proud to say that I froze in shock at how casually he said it. Before I had the chance to say anything, Eve stood up and said, "In my opinion, you're an asshole who needs to take his patients more seriously instead of judging them."

"There's no reason for language like that, young lady," the doctor said, almost confused, like she was being unreasonable.

I stood up and put a hand on Eve's arm. She was shaking with anger. "Doctor, I came here for your professional opinion, not your personal one. Please make sure my files get to my family doctor. *He* respects his patients and is a professional."

I took Eve's hand and left the office with my aching head held high.

We were quiet until we got to the car, then she said, "How could *you* be so calm?"

I did my best to not take the emphasis on "you" personally. "You're different, aren't you. I don't mean weird or neurodivergent. I mean you're magic or something," I blurted out.

Confused, she said, "What? Why do you say that?" Her guarded attitude would have been adorable if it hadn't been so heartbreaking.

"I don't know how you've been doing it, but you've been healing me. I know you have. You're probably the only reason I have any vision left, right?" I tried to sound appreciative instead of terrified.

"Yes," she said, looking down and not volunteering any information.

"That sounds lonely. I'm sorry you have to keep this secret, and I don't want you to tell me anything unless you are ready." I took her hand and kissed her palm before adding, "Thank you for trusting me."

Tears rolled down her face, and I wanted to fight the world for what it had done to her. With a small hitch in her voice, she finally asked, "But what does that have to do with the doctor?"

"A lot of doctors are asses, especially to girls. When I had tonsillitis at seven, one doctor suggested I had overburdened my vocal cords by talking too much. I'm kind of used to it, but I will be filing an online complaint."

Giving a small chuckle, she asked, "So where to?"

It was almost lunch so I replied, "Let's get some fast food breakfast and head back to school. I have a quiz in biochem if we can reach the teacher."

I tried calling my mom again and got her answering machine. I left a message and turned back to Eve. "Who do you suggest?"

"Normally, I'd call Jason and Kennedy, but they're already here."

"They don't strike me as regular government agents. Who are they really?"

Eve had pain in her eyes and then shook her head. "It's not my secret to tell." She paused and then said, "I can call Jason's sister from a payphone. She might know what to do."

We drove to the nearest A&W and got lucky with a payphone near their washrooms. Eve called and had a quick talk explaining everything to a woman's voice on the phone. When she was done and we were waiting for our order, I asked, "So?"

"She said she trusted Jason and Kennedy to get out of anything and that if they weren't back in two days, she'd send someone to look into it."

I gave a low whistle and said, "You told her everything, and she wasn't phased or even worried about him?"

Giving a chuckle, Eve replied, "Jason and Kennedy have been through a lot. They're strong, resourceful, and lucky. I'm sure they're fine."

We got our food and I considered telling her about my dream, but I wasn't Percy Jackson: I didn't get prophetic dreams.

As we ate, I said, "The etching on your flute isn't an indigenous design is it? It's got too many sharp corners, more of an African vibe, but not quite that either."

"How did you know?"

"I tried researching it to see if it had meaning to the tribes in Vancouver. It's from your people, isn't it?" I had just told her I wouldn't press, but I was curious.

She sighed and said, "Yeah. My father should have taught me to carve the flute when I turned twelve. But since he's dead, my adoptive mother found an elder in Vancouver who was willing to teach me. It's not exactly the same kind, but close enough."

I nodded. I wanted to ask a million other questions, but instead I ate another onion ring.

We took the same way back that we'd taken there, but we were stopped by a new barricade. A different soldier met us and his bright green eyes and fuzziness to my sight told me he was one with the goo. When he saw me, he just smiled, winked and motioned us to drive through.

"I guess the One is back in business, but why didn't it try to attack us?" I asked, as much to myself as Eve.

We stopped at the diner on the way and picked up coffees for Eve, me, and Mr. Smith.

The diner was almost empty and the streets were like a ghost town. As we drove through, it was eerily quiet.

"Where is everyone?" Eve asked as we pulled into the student parking. There were no other cars.

I sighed and said, "I have a bad feeling about this."

"Bad sick or bad psychic?"

I laughed and said, "Bad, as in I've seen too many horror movies."

Nodding sagely, she got out of the car. I followed and we headed to Mr. Smith's office. There was an undignified yelp when I knocked on the door.

"Miss Benson! Do you know where everyone is?" When he saw the coffee, he smiled and said, "Oh, thank you."

"I don't. I had a doctor's appointment and came back here after."

"Bah. Some sort of prank I'm sure. I'll give Principal Moore a piece of my mind when he comes in for letting the staff do this. Whatever, I have a lot of paperwork to get to anyway." He sounded hurt as he saw all the papers mixed with trash.

"Okay. I'm going to head to class."

"No point. Well, maybe your teleconference will work. It's hard wired anyway." As we left, I thought I heard him crying. I never know what to feel when I hear an adult cry. This time I just felt sad.

"What does he mean by hard wired?" Eve asked me.

"Alcohol with stimulants in it," I deadpanned. When she shook her head in confusion I said, "I don't know. When the teleconference rooms were built, they ran wires directly to them. Probably cable internet or DSL or something."

Eve didn't seem convinced.

We found Dean sitting outside the class with his hat on while he read a book. When he saw us, his usual cocky smile was replaced by one of relief. "Am I fucking glad to see you." He stood up and checked my eyes. "Good, you're not one of them."

"No, and neither are you or Mister Smith. Why have we been spared?" I asked. I assumed that Eve was protected by her healing powers but what about the rest?

"Hell if I know," he replied.

The beeping sound meant it was time for class to start, and we all went into the small room. Eve sat next to me and after a few clicks we had Doctor Batudev on screen.

"Hello class. I hear things are a little strange up there," he said.

"Very weird," I said dryly.

"Hi, Tommy," Eve said.

"Hi Evanna. Nice to see you. Okay, this line won't last forever. A friend is hacking through the Elmsley communications block. Tell me everything that is going on. In detail." He didn't seem nervous, but his brow was furrowed and he was fidgeting with a pencil.

The three of us told him everything.

"Wow." He paused before saying, "I've never known Kennedy and Jason to give up or fail. But just in case, you need to figure out what you three, and anyone else who isn't affected, have in common."

In a thin voice, Dean asked, "Is there any way to analyse what this goo is?"

"Not easily, especially not with what you have available. I know someone that works with the science division of Elmsley. I'll see if she can tell me anything. They must have done tests." His image flickered out and he quickly added, "For now, find out why you haven't been affected. That will be the key to—"

"To what? Fight this? Save people?" I asked the blank screen loudly before swearing a lot. After a while, I just flopped back into my chair.

"Are you okay?" Dean asked.

"No!" I screamed. I knew it wasn't his fault, but I was angry. "I have no idea what the hell is going on. Most of the town is controlled by some sort of goo that wants me to join it, or maybe just to kill me. I can't reach my mom. I'm having headaches and seeing things and everyone keeps saying I need to let the sexy agents deal with it. I'm scared, I'm angry, and I just want to get the fuck out of this town." I leaned forward and rested my head on the cool desk.

Eve's hand on my back was cool and soothing while still sending sexy tingles all down my spine. "Let's try to figure out what we all have in common."

We talked about what we could have in common, but there was very little that didn't involve school. Dean didn't even like coffee, which I tried not to judge.

"It doesn't make any sense," Dean said, his macho facade giving way to a whine. I wanted to comfort him, but I couldn't think of what to say. "I need a smoke." He pulled out a brownish cigarette case that was starting to turn green.

"What's that?" I asked, pointing at the case.

He seemed surprised and said, "It's a cigarette case. My great-grandfather made it. He was a smith in town when it was first founded."

"Why is it turning green?" The case was like the negative image of the goo-people's auras.

"It's just a little tarnished. Copper does that. I need to polish it." He pulled out a cigarette.

"Please don't smoke in here," Eve said, sounding distracted.

"Fine. I need to go make sure my family is still okay despite most of the town being goo zombies." His moment of vulnerability was replaced by his mask of toughness.

"We should go talk to Allison. Her pumpkin was called 'Copper Tarnish' from an old folk story. Copper Tarnish sounds like what you're seeing in your auras."

We saw no one in the school, but in the parking lot and in the streets, there were people just shambling around aimlessly.

"This is creepy," I said.

Allison lived just outside of town in a small wooden house that had a large barn she used as a workshop. Everything was made of ornately carved wood.

"I'm getting the witch from *Brave* vibes from this place," I said as we drove up.

"I don't think we need to worry about your mom being turned into a bear. I guess I would have to be transformed." We parked and climbed out of the car. After she closed the door, she leaned on the roof and said, "Would you still like me if I were a bear?"

I leaned over on the other side and reached my hand out, a perk of a small car, and said, "Sweetie, I'm bi. I have nothing against bears."

We both blushed and laughed. It was nice being able to be both goofy and sexual with her without feeling like she was going to judge me.

"How can I help you two?" Allison sounded amused. "Or did you need more time to flirt?" She had a large grin on her face. Her grey hair was tied up in a messy bun, and she was wearing a long flowing dress with a flower pattern on it.

Trying to reign in my blushing wasn't easy, but I managed and said, "Do you know about the weird stuff going on in town?"

"Old weird or new weird? 'Cause if it's new I haven't been in town since the pumpkin carving contest. Congrats by the way. I've been too busy carving pumpkins for people, although no one's come to pick any up today."

"New weird. Thank you, but your pumpkin was better. As usual."

"No one appreciates true art. They only want cheap thrills, sex, and violence." She sighed and added, "Can't blame them, that stuff's pretty good too."

I tried not to laugh. She was either very bad at being bitter or trying to be funny. "I wanted to know more about your pumpkin and the Copper Tarnish story you based it on. I think it's related to what's going on."

Allison checked us both out and gestured for us to come in. "That's the kind of story that needs coffee, tea, or rum."

We all sat with fresh muffins and large cups of my mom's cinnamon coffee. Allison seemed distant for long enough that I thought she wasn't going to speak. Then she sighed and said, "This is the third town to sit here. I'm sure you've heard of Montrock and how everyone from town just disappeared one day in the early 1920s. But there was a town here before that.

"Despite there not being any real roads, the town of Djedi's Fall was here before. It was mostly a trapper village with a small mine. All the trading was done on the Abitibi river."

"When was this?" asked Eve, enthralled.

"There are no records of when the town was established, but it was active in the mid-1700s."

I felt like I knew where this was going and said, "I'm guessing Montrock was established in the early 1820s."

Allison beamed at me like a teacher who thought I was clever and added, "A few years later, they came up here and found Djedi's Fall completely abandoned."

"And no one knows why?" I was starting to think this was a waste of time.

"Nothing official, but my grandfather gave me a diary that belonged to the only survivor from Djedi's Fall, and in it he tells the story of the Copper Tarnish."

CHAPTER 12

The story, despite the buildup, was fairly simple. The men who worked the mines swore they saw a green liquid dripping from the walls and ceiling, but since no one but the miners had seen it, everyone assumed it was underground gas. This was so far back that it was easier for them to go through the caves blasting rather than use open pit mining.

They brought in birds to test the air as they dug, but nothing changed and soon a man disappeared. They thought he'd run off into the woods and assumed he'd die or come back, but then more and more men disappeared.

The town jumped to the usual conclusion that witches were taking the men. The accounts said that the men came back after a month, but they were changed with tarnished copper eyes and blood that flowed green.

The journal said that they tried shooting the miners, but they'd just get back up as if nothing had happened. Anyone who touched their blood was cursed to be just like them.

The diary said that he and his family had survived. In a desperate attempt to save himself, he loaded ore from the mines into his musket. When the monsters had been shot with the ore, they screamed, sizzled, and ran away.

When Allison finished her story, she asked, "Is it happening again?"

"Yes, but if copper stops them, we can just tell the military to shoot pennies at them," I said, only half joking.

Both Allison and Eve shook their heads. Allison said, "No, it's not the copper. It's something that is mixed with the copper, something unique to the area. The diary says that the miners all wore pure copper rings, and it had no effect."

"Also, Canadian pennies are less than five percent copper. Mostly they're made of steel with a little nickel in it," Eve said before correcting herself, "Unless they were made before 1996. Those were ninety-eight percent copper."

I told Allison everything that happened. It felt like so much, but it took a lot less time than expected. When I was done, she said, "Your professor is right. There has to be something that makes you resistant. I'm probably not infected because I haven't come in contact with anyone."

We all sat in silence. I tried to think about what could be causing our immunity. I didn't get far before Eve asked Allison a great question, "Since you knew about this, you must have prepared, right?"

The older woman was sheepish as she said, "I'm an artist who loves nature and likes folklore. I'm not Sarah Connor. I never really believed it was real. I assumed it was an elaborate joke or that there was a scientific explanation. Northern Ontario is rife with monster folklore, but none of it is real." Her face fell and she blanched. She must have been thinking of all the folk stories she'd read or heard. "I hope."

The sun was starting to set and I knew that even in a monster apocalypse, there would still be people at the diner and I had a shift to get to. "Thank you," I said and started to get up.

"Why don't you two stay here? My doors are made of thick wood and I have plenty of food. We could wait this out and let the military and police take care of it." There was panic in her voice. "I should have had decaf."

"Coffee!" I exclaimed.

"Did you want more?" Allison asked, her confusion winning over her fear.

"No. The coffee. If it's the copper, my mom used local metals to make her roaster. It must have some of the copper, and it's imparting that protection through the coffee."

Eve seemed like she really wanted to believe me but wasn't sure. "What about Dean?"

"His cigarette holder is made of copper and is really old, right?" Eve nodded and seemed to think about it. "It explains why we're okay and why the diner regulars are fine too."

"But Mister Smith?" Eve asked and then answered her own question, "Has almost as much of your mom's coffee as you do." She paused to think and said, "It's as good an answer as any. How do we prove it?"

"Girls!" exclaimed Allison. When we turned to her, I could see the fear in her eyes. "I'd like you to leave now."

"What happened to us staying here?" Eve asked. There was a sadness in her tone and maybe bitterness.

"I think you two are too connected to this, and I want nothing to do with it. I'm sorry." She sounded like she was about to cry.

Allison ushered us out and I heard her lock her door. It was made of heavy wood and would hold up like she said, as long as the goo-people didn't realize that the windows were better entry points.

As we went to the car, I said, "We need to get into my mom's roastery. It's a sealed off room with venting to the outside. It's locked, but I know where she keeps the keys." I checked my watch and added, "After my shift."

Visibly baffled, Eve said, "Does your shift really matter?" She leaned with her back against the driver door and I leaned against her.

"The regulars aren't affected, and it would be cruel of me to leave the others short-staffed, even in an apocalypse."

Eve pulled me closer and kissed me. Just as I was getting happily distracted, she pushed me off and said, "You act like a big bitch with everyone, but you're really a big softy aren't you?"

"I'm a reformed mean girl turned outcast. I hate the world, and the world hates me."

She gave a little giggle and said, "I don't hate you."

I kissed her again and stopped to say, "I'm glad. I don't hate you either, my queen."

In a whisper, she replied, "It's princess, but you can refer to me as your royal highness." She punctuated the last few words by flipping our positions and pinning me to the car.

We stopped talking, and after a few blissful seconds, I stopped thinking about anything but her lips and her hands on my body. We might have spent the rest of the night making out against my car if we hadn't been interrupted by a loud howl that seemed to transition into a chirping sound.

"That didn't sound like a wolf," I said breathlessly.

Eve went completely white. I saw the same fear in her eyes as I'd seen in Allison's: primal and hunted. "We need to go," she said in a shaky voice.

As Eve drove my mini back toward Ansonville, I couldn't help but glance over at her and her blonde curly hair as she was being bathed in the bright red of October's sunset. It was barely six, but the sun was going down quickly.

"Do I have something in my hair?" she asked, smiling innocently. The light flickered as the forest came closer to the road.

"What was that all about? What was that noise?" I asked. "I think you playing innocent is cute normally, but not with this. That was a terrifying noise."

She sighed, and it came out jagged and pained. "When I was young, there was a coup on my planet. I escaped here when I was still in diapers with the woman I grew up thinking of as my mother. When I was five, I started having nightmares about these creatures chasing me."

"Okay. I have lots of questions, but please go on." I was excited to learn all about her. I found myself wanting to explore everything she was as much as I wanted to explore every millimetre of her body. Somehow that surprised me more than her being an alien.

"I don't remember all the details, but we went on vacation to Whistler with Eddy, my mom's friend. I woke up screaming the second night and Eddy came to my room." I made a face and she corrected, "Oh! No, not like that! He was a nice man. He tried to comfort me, but just as he was explaining that monsters don't exist, I heard one of those howls." She shivered at the memory.

I patted her shoulder awkwardly. It's really hard to comfort someone who's driving.

"They're called Hunters: genetically engineered to be the perfect predator. They will hunt their prey across the universe. The next thing we knew, it broke down my door, and before Ed could do anything, it cut him in half. I can still hear the sound. A sickening squelch." She was crying, and I desperately wanted to find this creature and rip its head off.

With a deep breath, she continued, "I thought I was going to die, but it leaned over me and sniffed before saying in a hissing voice that was punctuated with clicks, 'I have hunted you a long time, little princess. Tonight, you join an elite group of kills.'"

"Holy shit. That's how you found out you were a space princess? How did you survive?"

"My mom showed up just as the Hunter stopped talking and grabbed it by the head, burning it from the inside." She seemed relieved to be done with the story, but still shaken.

"Wow. How did she burn it? With a flare?"

With a little giggle that sounded more tired than amused, Eve said, "Earth is called a death world by the rest of the universe. It's the only planet with big predators. You also have more extreme weather, more disease, and horrifying things like parasites. Because of that, the rest of the universe evolved faster than humans, and we developed genetic manipulation that gave every race and class special powers. My ancestors got healing. My mom's ancestors got the ability to shoot flames from their hands."

"Okay, but what about the Hunter? If you had no large animals, how do they exist?" I felt like I was prying, but I was extremely curious.

"They aren't animals. They're sapient like you and me, but instead of getting something like healing, they were changed to become the ultimate killers."

We could see the lights of the diner now, and I was relieved. I kept expecting to see one of the Hunters lurking in the dark of the forest next to the highway. It didn't help that my head was pounding out the *Jaws* theme and my vision was getting hazy again.

She stopped the car in front of the diner and turned to me. I reached out and grabbed her the second she unbuckled her seatbelt. I hugged her tight and said, "Thank you for trusting me. I really appreciate it."

"You're the first person I've ever told. I didn't even tell Kennedy. I feel like a useless princess."

"You're not useless, you've saved me at least twice this week. I—" I'm not sure what I was going to say but it was cut off by a large explosion and smoke coming from the downtown area. "We should go check that out," I said.

"No. You have your work. I'll go check it out. My aunt— Well, if I have to be honest, she's a friend of Kennedy's, not really my aunt. That looked like it was close to her house." She raised her hand over her eyes to block the sun and said, "Someone could be hurt. I'll be careful, and I'll have my walkie-talkie the whole time."

We kissed and I pulled away before I decided I had to go with her. "Be safe."

I went into the diner and went through my regular routine of punching in, drinking coffee, chatting, and cleaning.

An hour passed quickly, and I was getting more worried about Eve. Unfortunately, there was nothing I could do even if I wanted to run out after her. She wasn't a fairy tale princess, just an alien one, and she definitely didn't need an over-caffeinated knight. I also couldn't drive, and she had my car. With my luck, she'd come to the diner while I was out looking for her.

As I took people's orders, my mind wandered, and I realized how ridiculous it seemed to have gone from running away from monsters, to investigating urban legends, to dealing with my job. It felt like I should be rushing out to do something or tell someone. But without the phones, I couldn't contact the military, the police were no help, and I had no idea what else to do.

My thoughts were interrupted when Fred arrived at the diner. "Fred? We just saw you two nights ago? Everything okay?"

"Glad you're worried about me." He smiled and took a seat at the counter. "With all those government folks checking trucks and getting in people's business, I thought I should stick around a little until they got bored."

Mom and I had often jokingly debated what Fred was really transporting. There's no way coffee and random items kept him in business. We agreed it's something illegal, but not on what. She said drugs, but I thought something more sinister, like illegal organs or bombs.

I was really tempted to ask him, but then I remembered that trucks have radios. "Fred? Have you been able to talk to anyone on your radio?"

"Nope. Tried when my cell went dead, but I have nothing but the other truckers in town. Radio, cell, satellite phone, and everything else is blocked. Might as well have a beer with dinner."

"You always have a beer with dinner," I said teasingly.

"Now I don't have to feel guilty about it."

There was a lull in customers, and I was able to think and worry about Eve. I was just wondering if I should leave and go searching for her when she arrived frazzled. I put down the half empty coffee pot on the table I was cleaning and ran to hug her.

Taking her into the kitchen, I made her a coffee from a fresh pot and asked, "What happened?"

Jordan saw us and his eyes got big. "Should I leave?" he asked, never taking his eyes off Eve.

"No, it's okay. Just pretend I'm not here." Eve's reply would have seemed odd before today. She continued, "I went to see my aunt. No sign of what the explosion was and the smoke stopped before I got downtown. So I went into my aunt's house, and she started yelling at me about God. It took me a little time to realize she was talking about us. She gave me the whole argument from Leviticus onward. It was terrible. I knew she'd taken to religion, but this was worse than ever. She grabbed me by the arm and tried to drag me to church to repent my sins."

I didn't know what to say. I was surprised by Jordan replying, "That doesn't sound like her."

"It wasn't. As we were leaving the house I saw her eyes and it was bright enough to see they were green instead of brown." I gasped and Jordan frowned, confused. "I pulled away from her, and she made this noise like an old-time modem combined with a Ringwraith." She stopped and took a drink of coffee. The warm liquid seemed to settle her nerves.

"The coffee really does help," she muttered before continuing, "They all just came out of their houses and shambled toward me. I ran to the car and drove as fast as I could, but they were everywhere."

I suddenly had a really bad feeling. I ran to the front and saw that Fred was locking the doors. When he saw me, he said, "I think we have a problem. I recommend barricading the doors."

Outside, I could see half the town surrounding the building, all of them with the telltale blurriness of being gooed.

There weren't too many people in the diner; Jordan, Eve, Fred, an older couple I didn't know, John a trucker, and a man in the furthest booth that I couldn't see clearly.

Everyone except the man in the farthest booth helped lock and barricade the doors and exposed windows. Unfortunately, the majority of the front was windows.

"Why aren't they moving?" Fred asked. He was right, the entire population was just standing outside the diner scowling and evil-looking.

"It's like they're waiting for something," I said.

The man in the far booth stood up and started to clap. I hadn't focused on him closely enough and I should have. He was blurry, but in such an intense way that I could barely see him. It was only by seeing his reflection in the glass of the coolers that I recognised him.

"I really can't believe how hard the One has tried to absorb you. It's almost comical how much it's failed, despite two months of trying." Harold stared right at me, and his eyes were still the same shade of piercing amber and not green. He glowed red and he was a little fuzzy, like those taken by the goo.

"You're not part of the One?" I asked, trying to buy time for me to figure out what was going on.

He laughed. "The One is weak. It only wants to eat this town and be left alone. It doesn't understand the power it wields or the strength it could have. Why kill all the humans when you can control them?"

"Okay Doctor No-way-in-hell, what's going on?"

"To put it in terms you can understand, I rebooted the One and have taken over. It's now my tool." He paused for dramatic effect, but it just came off as awkward. He wasn't a great performer. "Now, if you'll be so kind as to drop your protective wards and let my friends in, I can take you back to my lab and find out what makes you tick. Or I can rip everyone here apart and still take you to my lab."

Chapter 13

“Okay, first of all, I can’t believe I kissed you. Second, what the hell are wards? And lastly, I’m not big on the whole dissection plot.”

Fred glared at Harold like he was an annoyance and beyond useless. “If you think I’ll let you dissect my favourite waitress, you’re in trouble.”

“What are you going to do, hit me with your truck?”

“No, I’ll just shoot you.” Fred pulled out a handgun. It was like the ones detectives used on old television shows, nothing as sophisticated or flashy as the laser guns from the last shootout.

“I’m a wizard and a biologist that has merged himself into the most powerful entity on the planet. Guns won’t stop me.”

It was starting to be like a bad reproduction of an even worse western: *Midnight at the Dancing Goat.*

The building was surrounded by goo-people, the angry man in the diner was ready to kill everyone who stood in his way, and we were cowering in a corner. What we needed was a diversion. No, what we needed was backup.

“Harold, there’s no reason to kill anyone. Just turn the communications back on, and we can get you a better hostage than me. Why would you want me when you can have the prime minister or something?” I was expecting a monologue, God, this guy liked to talk, but instead he seemed worried.

“I turned off the communications so you couldn’t call in reinforcements. Why would I turn them back on?”

Leaning over to me and speaking softly, Eve said, “He’s lying.” Her soft voice and the scent of her so close gave me good shivers. There my body went again, going for horny over panic.

We were alone, no help to call for, he hadn't turned off the communications, which meant someone else had. Probably the military people, but it could also have been the alien assassins – or was there another group trying to make my life hard?

"Helen, come here now!" Harold ordered.

I stood up and started moving toward him before I realized what I was doing. Fred reached out a hand but missed me. I internally screamed at my body to listen to my commands and it refused. I just kept moving. I couldn't stop. Reaching out, I grabbed at the closest thing I could. I threw salt and pepper shakers, plates, napkin holders, and even a knife. Nothing seemed to hurt him, although I was impressed that I hit him every time.

As I passed the table I'd been cleaning when Eve arrived, I picked up the abandoned pot of coffee. It was an old style glass one, and I hoped the coffee was hot enough to hurt him if we were wrong about its effects. I threw the pot, and it shattered with a satisfying crash.

At first Harold was smug, but then the coffee started to sizzle and burn him. He screamed and all the goo-people stopped moving. The coffee couldn't have been that hot which meant we'd been right about its effects. I regained control over my feet and stopped moving.

He screamed something about my sexuality and being a bitch, but I wasn't listening. I turned, grabbed Eve's hand, and ran toward the kitchen. "Come on," I yelled as the others just stared at us. I didn't need to tell them twice. We all ran for the exit door in the kitchen.

After the panic and fear inside, the complete stillness outside was unnerving. The goo zombies had just stopped moving, and it seemed all of nature was holding its breath. No cars passed, no wind blew. The silence was physically imposing.

The older couple ran for their car. I watched them, expecting something to jump out, but they made it to the car and drove away, never giving us a second glance.

"That will haunt them for the rest of their lives," Fred said, still holding his gun. With a shrug, he added, "We need to move." I'd lost track of John at some point and Jordan was following us.

Gesturing back to the building, I said, "We need to get into my mom's roastery."

Fred seemed unsure, but followed Eve and I. The outside door to the roasting room was solid steel and would be more appropriate on a bank. I fished the key from my pocket and opened the door.

"You got the key?" Eve asked.

"Yeah, my mom kept it in her sock drawer along with her porn magazines."

Eve blushed, Jordan shuffled uncomfortably, and Fred chuckled.

The inside of the roastery was a little bit of a let down. Nothing super cool inside, just three massive storage shelves, one with green beans, one with roasted and labelled beans by flavour, and another with large vats of flavouring. In the middle of the room were two machines, one large gas-powered roaster that could do sixty kilograms and another that was effectively a large fan inside a bowl that cooled the beans and sucked out the excess chaff.

When I got close, I could see that the roaster had veins of copper running through the whole thing.

"There's copper in here, but I was expecting something more magical," I said and sat down on the floor.

Eve started to explain everything to Fred and Jordan, leaving out the parts where I was being affected and she was an alien princess.

When she was done, Fred said, "Wow. Nothing like Northern Ontario for weird shit or drama."

Jordan sat next to me and pulled out a pair of glasses with small round lenses. "Try these on. I bought them from a travelling wizard a few years ago."

I put them on and my vision swam. It was like seeing auras, but everywhere. When I got used to all the glowing and colours, I started to see formulas and words written on everything.

Jordan gestured and said, "These are wards. They're permanent magical effects that are used to enhance or protect things. Your mom uses this room to make coffee, but also to enhance its flavour and make it heal people a little."

"How does she do that?" I asked.

"Your mom is what we call an adept. She has access to a little bit of magic and uses it in her everyday life. It's what humans in olden times called a 'hedge witch'." Jordan sounded perfectly comfortable talking about magic.

Eve beat me to the question I wanted to ask, "What's the difference between a wizard and an adept?"

Surprisingly, it was Fred who answered, "Wizards are like heavy-weight fighters, all strength and technique. Adepts are more like judo fighters who leverage the things around them to do the same thing. Basically, wizards have so much magic they don't need to be as careful, while adepts have to be super careful because they have so little."

"Does that mean I'm an adept?" I asked.

Jordan and Fred shook their heads, and Fred answered, "No, unlike Jordan here and your freaky admirer goo-overlord, being an adept is not genetic." I guess that meant Fred knew about aliens too. "Aliens and wizards pass on their powers, adepts don't." Yup, he definitely knew.

"How did you know Harold was a wizard?" I asked, having trouble digesting everything. My pounding headache wasn't helping either. "Who's screaming?"

Eve sat down next to me and put her hand on my head. "She's warm. I think her mom's coffee has been holding back the goo, but she's having trouble fighting it. Especially with that jerk taking control." Her hands sent pleasurable and calming shivers down my whole body, but it wasn't enough.

Open the door, Harold's voice was in my head and he was angry. Everything became tinted green, and I stood up. Unlike earlier, I didn't want to stop. This was what I was supposed to be doing.

I made it to the door and opened it. There was a scream of anger, frustration, and pure hatred in my head, but I couldn't tell if it was mine or not.

I vaguely heard Eve yelling at me, but I pushed her aside gently and swung the door open. Harold's smile made me happy. He seemed proud and I desperately wanted to believe it was because of me.

Harold's hand raised a chef's knife. I vaguely recognized it from the diner's kitchen. He swung the knife downward like someone desperately pretending to be a samurai. In that moment, I knew the knife was meant for me, and I felt blessed to be dying for Harold.

The knife didn't connect with me. Eve stepped in front of it, using her arm to push me back. Harold's swing connected just below her elbow. He must have been super strong, because the cut severed her arm off completely.

Eve screamed and blood sprayed everywhere. An 80s slasher would have thought the quantity was over the top. She soaked me and Harold. I even got some in my mouth. The moment I tasted her blood, my mind cleared, and I started to gag.

I didn't see Fred take off his belt, but suddenly, it was around what was left of Eve's arm.

While Eve's blood seemed to have cleared my head it didn't do anything for Harold. He was just as angry, but I couldn't hear his thoughts anymore. I still heard the distant screaming, and I knew it wasn't me.

Without thinking, I moved forward and prepared to punch Harold as hard as I could. I stopped when a shot rang out and a part of Harold's face flew off. He turned as if it was nothing more than a papercut and ran toward John the trucker, who was standing obviously petrified. Another five shots rang out and made squelching noises when they hit Harold. He howled and ran away.

John was a big broad man with bright red hair that was just starting to go white. He was tough and in control normally, but right then he was like a terrified child. He swore in full paragraphs before walking over to the entrance of the roastery. As he got to the door, he stepped on Eve's arm and tripped, falling onto his back into the blood.

A howl that didn't sound quite terrestrial echoed through the quiet night.

Fred moved toward the other trucker and said, "That sounds like something we don't want to deal with. Get in here."

John's eyes grew wide. He took Fred's help and joined us inside. I closed the door again and realized that I had stood there the entire time. My friend, maybe girlfriend, was bleeding out behind me, a poor trucker was almost killed, and I was still just standing there gaping and covered in drying blood.

"Eve, are you okay?" I asked.

"'Tis but a scratch." She had a smile as she quoted the Black Knight from *Monty Python and the Holy Grail*.

I couldn't remember the reply to it, but it was something about having your arm cut off. "Wow. Dark." It was the only thing I could think of saying.

Eve smirked and waved her stump at me. I was starting to think the blood loss was getting to her when I saw her arm. Like a new branch from a tree, a small forearm and hand was growing out of her stump.

"I'll heal, it's okay," she said, trying to reassure me.

"First off, are you part starfish? Second, it's not fair that you get a limb chopped off and have to comfort me."

Putting the back of her good hand on her forehead, she deadpanned, "Oh no. I might faint."

I rolled my eyes and moved forward to catch her. She seemed impossibly light in my arms. "Are you also lighter than most people?"

"No. I think you're just really strong. Remember you threw me across the room?"

"Oh right. Sorry again." I couldn't stop staring at the slowly growing arm.

Eve gave a small giggle and said, "You can put me down and make it up to me with some food. This is really draining, and if I don't eat, I might actually pass out."

"My mom is a notorious snacker. Let me look around." I searched more thoroughly and found a large bag of mini chocolate chip cookies.

Eve made grabby hands, one normal and one still growing, and ripped the top off the cookie bag. She proceeded to do the most authentic Cookie Monster impression I've ever seen.

Jordan was the first to speak and said, "That was a two-kilogram bag of cookies." There was awe in his voice.

"Not very princessy of me, I guess."

No one answered her, and eventually John asked, "What's going on?"

"Northern Ontario, man," Fred said it as if it explained everything, and John just sat down and nodded.

John said, "I think I might want to get a safer route, like through a warzone."

Fred chuckled but there was something haunted behind the laughter.

Eve stood up and stretched. Both her arms were the same now except for the jagged cut to her sweater where the arm had been lopped off and a surprisingly little amount of blood. Most of it had been propelled outward.

"Are you okay?" I asked. I didn't like being worried. I much preferred being angry.

"I'm okay. Still very hungry. I'm going to need something high in protein." Her normally Zen and borderline spacey expression was now hungry.

"It's been a while. I think Harold is actually gone this time. He didn't like your blood."

Eve nodded and said, "Yeah. It has certain healing and cleansing properties. I don't think it interacted well with whatever spell he used to bond with the goo."

"Is that why my head is clearer than it's been in over a week?" I asked, suddenly self-conscious about the amount of blood on me.

"Yes. I'm really hungry. Let's get out of here."

John, who'd been sitting still, suddenly stood up and bolted for the door.

"Wait," both Fred and Jordan said at the same time. John didn't listen and threw open the door, not waiting before running out.

I held my breath and was just about to let it out when the Hunter appeared in front of John.

It was like a dark grey crab with four legs and an elongated body. Its head jutted out from a stalk on its chitinous body.

John turned and froze when he saw it. The head had no eyes, but as it swept from side to side, dozens of holes that must have been for smelling or hearing, closing and opening. It stopped and seemed to focus on the statue of John and its holes gave off a yellow light that pulsed like random sparkle lights.

There was no warning when it lashed out with one of its scythe-like legs. The slash cut John cleanly in two. I knew I'd have nightmares about seeing the man's insides leak out of his still-standing corpse before it knew any better than to collapse.

It smelled him, and I heard a faint clicking noise like someone rhythmically typing on a loud keyboard. It seemed to find him offensive because it slashed him up a few more times and leaned its entire body into the blood trail that Harold had left. It followed the trail back to the door and the clicking was so loud it hurt my ears.

It smelled the ground in front of the door before opening its head like a disturbing alligator and eating the arm that was still on the ground.

I was sure at that point that we were doomed. I wanted to slam the door shut but I was frozen in terror. I held my breath and watched as it smelled the door and tried to come into the room. A pink glow of energy that vaguely smelled like coffee roasting stopped it from entering. Its head swung from side to side as it clicked in a random pattern, the lights that came out of its head glowed in a semi-random pattern. In a breathy almost clicking voice, I heard it say, "Princess!"

Finally after what felt like days, it turned away from the door and followed the path that Harold had taken.

The four of us stood there trying hard not to breathe until we heard the howl. It was far away, or far enough to make us braver.

"What the fuck are we going to do?" I asked finally, my voice shrill in the silence.

"You are going to go home and cook this girl a meal," Jordan replied. "Your mom warded the apartment, and you should be safe there until this is all over."

"What about you?" I asked.

Solemnly Jordan said, "I'm going to my place. I paid a wizard a few years ago to ward it, and it should be good. Fred, you want to bunk with me until this blows over?"

Smiling, Fred said, "Why Jordan, we barely know each other, buy me a drink first." It was meant to be silly, but there was an edge of panic in his voice.

"I have some at home," Jordan said and winked. Were they awkwardly flirting or just being silly? I couldn't tell.

I looked over to where John had been killed and was going to ask what we should do about him, but his body was gone.

Jordan and Fred walked us to my door, and we locked it behind us. I braced a chair against door again and finally asked, "How did you get in the other day? Can you teleport?"

"Nope. Your house key is on your car keys, and this carpet slips. I was able to push enough to squeeze in." She said the last part in an exaggerated husky voice and despite the trauma and horror of the night, my body reacted to it.

"Hey! Not fair using that voice when I'm literally covered in your blood. Let me shower first."

"Food first!" Eve said followed by: "Feed me!" in the same tone as Audrey from *Little Shop of Horrors*.

CHAPTER 14

E ve's eyes were seductive, and with the night I'd had, I wanted nothing but to lose myself in everything that was her. However, after a steak dinner for her and some chicken nuggets for me, she was ready to fall asleep.

She washed herself off in the sink and curled up on the couch. She was asleep before I managed to find the blanket and put it on her.

I stood for a moment, watching her sleep. There was something sweet and serene about her that I never saw when she was awake. It made me sad that under that spacey, seemingly carefree facade was a sad and anxious girl. I wanted to take all that away from her and keep her safe.

First, I needed to clean her blood out of my hair. The dark brown of dried blood did not go with my bright red. A hot shower relaxed me, and I finally started to feel tired too.

By the end of the shower, I was back to fighting a headache. I did the only sensible thing and made myself a pot of extra strong coffee.

With a metal carafe and a large cup, I sat on the floor in my mother's study and decided to check out her books on the occult. Everyone's mothers have a large shelf of occult and mythology books, right? I remembered sitting on the same floor as a kid, taking in all the pictures of beasts, witches, castles, tarot cards, and dragons. I loved dragons.

I rifled through the titles and found one called *The Worlde Magica* by J. A. Martin. The picture on the front was of an old man in wizard robes entertaining a small group of children with fireworks that came out of a crystal staff.

The book was obviously written for a younger audience with a fairly simple vocabulary. From the copyright, it said the book was originally published in 1894. I appreciated the simplicity of it at one in the morning. It was split into four sections: Wizards, Fay, Aethermen, and Others.

I recognized my mom's writing in the margins. She'd crossed out Aethermen and written in Aetherborn instead.

With all the talk about my mom being an adept, I decided to start with the wizard section. I know Fred said they were different, but magic users are magic users right?

There were almost no corrections except for the section on Merlin. The line, "A shadowy and untameable figure" was underlined three times. There was a useful definition of magic as the manipulation of Aether, or as my mom wrote, "magic stuff". It then defined Aether as, "the force of chaos that assails our universe" and could only be effectively wielded by wizards.

The next section seemed to be all about fairy creatures apparently ruled by a powerful lord called Robin, who was both a trickster and a ruler. I guess Shakespeare was half wrong. There were no corrections in this one.

In the Aetherborn section, every instance of Aethermen was corrected. It talked about mythical creatures that had the power of Gods but were created by wizards and sometimes by human imagination.

"I need to think about Naomi Scott and Tom Hiddleston more often," I mumbled. Next to the words, "power of gods" was written, "Mr. Johnson?" I wondered if there was any relation to the Agents Johnson that I'd been dreaming about since they disappeared. Next to the words, "created by wizards" my mom had written, "Banned in 1919 after what had happened during WWI." I both wanted to know and was terrified to find out.

The last section had short descriptions for a lot of different human-like creatures that weren't considered monsters or Aetherborn.

> ***Artificers:*** *Non-magical humans who use magical items and artifacts to mimic a wizard's power. Most are driven mad by the power.*
>
> ***Changelings:*** *Although often considered Aetherborn, they are*

creatures born of the desire to have a child. They are often odd and obsessive. They can learn any magic with enough exposure.
Ides: *Ladies of magic born of the elements. Few are left, and those that are, are powerful and terrifying.*

The next entry caught my attention:

"*Anima Loci:* Sometimes a place or element, through contact with the Aether, will develop magical properties and sapience." In bold red letters, my mom had written, "Old mines? Copper Tarnish?"

The last entry was for adepts. I wondered why the entries weren't in alphabetical order.

"Adepts: The weakest of magical talents. They are inconsequential." My mother drew a hand with the middle finger raised next to that one. She also wrote, "Adepts are experts at using small amounts of magic to big effect. They are the most organized of magic users and the only ones who cannot pass down their gifts to their children." There was a sad face after the last word. That seemed to confirm I wasn't an adept.

I stood up and stretched. I had finished the carafe and was starting to feel sleepy again. I went to the washroom where I swear I could have filled the carafe again. Coffee was delicious, but it went right through me.

As I washed my hands, I glanced at myself in the mirror. I was like a gaunt, tired, and almost sick version of my mom. I couldn't see my aura, however, and that bothered me. Was it just the coffee and Eve keeping me from going green, or was there something else?

Eve had rolled the blanket off of herself, so I covered her again. I sat down on the chair next to the couch and watched her some more. I considered practising the guitar but didn't want to move. It felt like my head was too full of new information, and I didn't know how to organize it.

Sleep is like a slasher movie villain, you can run, but eventually it'll catch up and get you. I don't remember falling asleep, but I did and in my dreams I saw the agents again, still tied up and covered in goo. Harold, who looked like he'd picked a fight with a kettle, his face was still bubbling from the cold coffee I'd thrown at him, was pacing and reading from a large leather book. He would randomly say something, and Richard would cock his head at him as if he didn't understand.

I was disembodied, which was a weird feeling, but I could feel the goo. It was fighting whatever magic Harold was trying to use on it. I could feel its confusion and its hunger. It wasn't hungry for food, but for understanding and experience. It felt young and curious more than ancient and evil.

A flash of pain hit me, and I woke up. The building was shaking and there was a loud noise.

"Earthquake!" screamed Eve, and she ran for a doorway.

I'd never felt an earthquake and my instinct was to go check the window, which was probably pretty dangerous. Outside, I saw a column of green fire coming from town.

"I don't think that's an earthquake," I said.

The shaking continued, and so did the noise. Eve asked, "What do you see?"

"A giant green flame going straight into the air," I replied, deadpan. Then in a more chipper tone, I said, "Coffee?"

We both laughed, and I went to the kitchen while Eve went into the washroom. When she came out, she asked, "Did you want to go find out what's going on with the fire?"

I handed her a travel mug of coffee and a croissant sandwich with peanut butter and jam and replied, "Yes, please."

I half expected there would be large gash marks on the outside door showing some epic struggle, but there was nothing but a thin layer of frost.

Winter was maybe two months away for most of the country, but it was reminding us that we only had a few weeks before the first full snowfall in Northern Ontario. I can only remember one year where there wasn't permanent snow on the ground by the second weekend of November.

Dawn was just about to break, which meant it was around seven in the morning. The diner, despite last night, had one waitress, a cook, and half a dozen patrons. Someone deserved a raise for cleaning up after the previous night.

"Why aren't there any goo-people waiting for us?" I asked as I got into the passenger seat.

"They stopped trying to catch you after you threw coffee at Harold. Maybe he hasn't regained full control of them again yet."

Eve started the car and I lifted my cup in a mock salute.

We followed the pillar of light like moths casually driving toward a flame. As we passed the school, I saw only Mr. Smith's car and no one around. I was sad and annoyed. I had been looking forward to today. It was the last day of school before Halloween, which meant we were allowed to go to class in costume.

"You seem sad. What are you thinking?" Eve asked, putting her hand on my knee and sending warm tingly feelings all over my body.

"I had the perfect costume planned out for school. I bought an old wedding dress from a thrift shop and splattered it with fake blood. I had a veil and a rubber axe to go with it." I pouted exaggeratedly.

Eve nodded seriously and said, "Constance Hatchaway from Haunted Mansion?"

"Yes!" I desperately wanted to know what she'd thought of dressing up as, but before I could ask, we reached the sight of the flames. I'm not sure what I was expecting, but a large barrel with green flames coming out of it in the middle of the road felt a little anticlimactic.

Dean was sitting on the curb off to the side smoking and fidgeting with his cigarette case. I rolled down my window and said, "So is this your giant inferno?"

He nodded, took a dramatic drag and flicked the cigarette into the flames. "It's a combination of high powered fuel with copper oxide. I was making it for my final project and when I tested it, all the goo-people ran away. So now my family is safe."

My jaw fell open and I said, "You made a giant repellent? How long will it last?"

He shrugged and said, "I have enough fuel to last a few days. You two want to bunk down with me until this all passes?"

I shook my head. At some point between last night and talking to him, I'd made a decision. "No. I'm sick of reacting, and I'm sick of feeling helpless. I'm going to do something about it."

"Hot," was all he said as he walked away and waved his hands around the flame.

Eve gave me a nod and I said, "Where to?"

"The Pioneer Museum!" I said enthusiastically.

She grinned and started to drive. When we got to a stop sign, she admitted to not knowing where it was.

The Ansonville Pioneer Museum was a staple of grade school field trips. It was a small building with lots of room, a musty smell, and old farming equipment in the front yard. I'd volunteered there for a few summers, helping to digitize their catalogues.

It was musty and boring, but they did have cotton candy, popcorn, and hot dog carts that they rented out. My dance studio had rented them more than once to raise money. I was pretty good at making a large cotton candy.

The back door was never locked. Janice, the curator and owner, didn't want to pay a locksmith. As we entered the office, I asked Eve, "Do you think Dean was using magic on the fire?"

"I don't know. I can't see magic or anything. It does seem improbable that he'd be able to keep a flame that big going for so long. What was his aura like?"

I had expected the question. "It's pink, just like my mom's."

I gave the squeaky door a hip check, and it opened. I went straight for the computer, which was not an official antique, but should be considered one. I pressed the on button and the fans began to roar. Turning on the old CRT monitor, I said, "This could take a while."

"Why are we here? Did you want to make out in a reproduction of an 18th century convenience store?" Eve asked, winking.

"I like the way your mind works," I said and had to fight the flush coming to my cheeks. "We're here for weapons. Once I get this thing started, I can search for anything made of copper from the mines."

The collection management system was simple enough, and once it was opened, I searched for copper. I found a few trinkets, a few commemorative plaques, and some coins. "This isn't going to help."

"What about bronze? Or brass? They're copper alloys," Eve asked.

"I don't know if an alloy would work," I said, but then added, "but why not."

We got lucky. The son Hank Anson, founder of Ansonville, was part of the light infantry and they'd commissioned a bronze replica of a British infantry sword. There was also a brass bedpost from some rich man's bed. We took both and a handful of coins before getting back into the car.

"To the mines?" Eve asked, not sounding confident.

I felt silly bringing this up, but I said it anyway, "I think we need coffee."

She laughed and said, "Of course we do." It wasn't condescending or mean; her laugh was nervous.

"I mean we need coffee to defend ourselves. I have a few water pistols at home and I think we could fill them with coffee and use them for defence. Bronze swords and bedposts are cool and all, but we know the coffee works." I felt sheepish. It was such a teen from a bad horror movie idea.

"That's a great idea. We should also get some to drink," Eve smiled and started to drive.

We were quiet until she parked outside the diner. I couldn't see John's bloodstains from where we parked, but I still knew they were still there.

"Eve. I th—"

"No!" Eve interrupted me. "I'm going with you. I am not staying behind and I refuse to let those damned monsters scare me anymore."

A flash of pain threatened to liquify my brain. I screamed. When it was over, I felt like something was different. The pressure on my mind was lessened.

"Harold has control of the One again," I said.

"How do you know?" Eve put her hand on my neck, and I felt some relief.

"Thank you. The pressure and anger I've been feeling changed. It's like the One was angry and wanted me to be part of it. Now it's angry, hungry, and oddly insecure. I think Harold is overpowering it."

Eve frowned and said, "I almost feel bad for the murderous goo."

I felt like there was something I was missing, but it was hard to concentrate. So I did what I always do when I can't control the situation, I went to the diner and had breakfast food.

We ate, brewed enough coffee for the large three litre carafes that my mom used for catering, and packed a lunch. We also retrieved the water pistols, and some other things I thought could be useful.

By the time we were done, the sky was already turning pink, but the air surprisingly felt warm compared to the wind. There was an odd quiet without any other cars on the highway. With the cold weather and everything happening, it seemed the animals were staying quiet too; there were no crows anywhere to be heard.

We arrived at the pit where the old mine had been, and parked next to three other cars, all rentals. The last of the daylight was quickly fading.

"You know it'll be pitch dark when we get to the cave," Eve said.

"I know. We're going to get there in the dark on the day before Halloween." I took out the sandwiches we'd brought. We'd agreed that eating an early dinner was a good idea in case one of us lost another limb.

"Would sound cooler if it was on Halloween proper," she said, smiling mischievously. She drank some coffee.

"Who knows? If we hurry this up, we could maybe make it to Dean's party," I said and we both knew that party wasn't going to happen. I waited to make sure she had swallowed her coffee and added, "Plus Halloween is great, but I prefer Eve's anyway."

She burst into giggles, stopping long enough to say, "That was cheesy."

"Sorry," I said, suddenly feeling really uncomfortable. Damn it, I really liked her, and now I was feeling really self conscious.

"Hey! Hey! No, cheesy is good. You make me laugh, you make me the best kind of uncomfortable. Don't go wherever it is you're going." She punctuated her words by kissing me.

It was tentative at first, but soon I was lost in the taste of her lips. Every touch was electric and hungry. I wanted to be as close to her as possible.

We pulled apart at the same time, and I could feel my lips tingling with overstimulation. I'd developed the habit of drinking coffee every time my mind felt fuzzy; this time it didn't work. Eve's effects weren't goo or magic, they were purely physical and emotional.

"I understand that your last relationships were crappy, but that's not your fault. They were cruel, and it's their fault." There was a defensive anger in her tone that made me feel protected. She was right, Richard and Veronica had done a real number on my self esteem.

Being accused of murder and becoming the town pariah while all my friends turned their backs on me hadn't helped.

Compared to all that, goo zombies and evil wizards weren't half as traumatizing.

"Thank you," I said and put my hand on her cheek. She took my hand and kissed each of my fingers. "Holy shit, Eve. I swear if you put a finger in your mouth, things are going to happen."

"What sort of things?" she asked in a husky voice.

"Sexy things!" I exclaimed breathlessly.

She smirked and let go of my hand. I wasn't thinking very clearly and didn't give my hand any commands. It proceeded to flop back into my lap like a dead fish.

"Something to remember if you're thinking of doing something reckless tonight," Eve gave me a stern glance.

"Point taken. Now let's go beat the shit out of three or four people that I've kissed."

Chapter 15

We went from the car, around the pit, and toward the caves. We were halfway there when Eve said, "Wait. Four?"

"Four what?" I'd forgotten what we'd talked about and had been focussing on the fact that there were no goo-people out here. If I was in charge, and I had a bunch of military guys under mind control, I'd have them guarding the entrance to my lair.

"You said three or four people you've kissed." Eve gave me a stern pout, which in the light of the waning moon was pretty sexy.

"I mean there's Richard, Veronica, and Harold." I would have counted on my fingers, but my hands were clutching a brass bedpost and a water pistol. "I don't know who else there is."

"Have you kissed that many people?"

"There was that one sleepover with the dance squad where we played spin the bottle just us girls," I said as seriously as I could.

"Really?" Eve asked incredulously.

I shook my head and said, "No, not really. I said three or four 'cause I thought it sounded cooler than saying three of the four."

A howl echoed through the pit, and I suddenly understood why there were no armed soldiers guarding the entrance.

"Let's keep moving," I said, seeing the terror on Eve's face.

We were almost at the entrance to the cave I'd gone into with Veronica so long ago, when Eve said, "Who's the fourth?"

I turned to her and her aura flickered from bright gold to bright green. I dropped everything I was holding and heard a crack of plastic breaking as the water gun hit the ground. I caught her before she fell and sort of collapsed underneath her.

It was dark, cold, and the night was clear. I sat in the former pit mine and held her. Her eyes flickered, and I could see the green winning. I grabbed the thermos from my backpack and poured some coffee into the lid for her. "You're the fourth. And the best. Sit up please," I asked, trying not to sound like I was begging.

"The One doesn't want me to. It has a message for you." She coughed and continued in the monotone voice I'd come to associate with the One, "You must help. He is contaminating..." Her aura became brighter green, and her face started to fuzz like the others.

I forced her to sit up and open her mouth, letting some of the warm coffee drip into it. She swallowed and nothing else happened. "*No!* Let her go. She's mine. Let her go or I will personally make sure that every millilitre of you is destroyed. Let her go or I will wage war on you and everything like you. Let her go!" I yelled and cried, ugly tears streaming down my face.

Through the haze of my tears, I couldn't see Eve's aura; I couldn't see much of anything. Between sniffles, Eve managed to turn and hug me. When I had cried enough to make myself feel weak, I wiped my tears away with the sleeve of my coat. Eve's aura was back to the golden glow that it had been before. My voice hitched as I said, "We forgot to bring tissues."

We both laughed and drank some of the coffee. Eve kissed me gently and then said, "Thank you."

"Don't thank me. I'm just glad you came back." I was scared by how hard it had hit me. I'd only met this girl a month ago and talked to her last week. What kind of sappy Hollywood heroine was I that I'd fallen this fast and this deep for the cute blonde curvy girl. She was a princess from space, so it's not like she wasn't extra special.

Both our water pistols had been cracked from the fall, but we still had a carafe of coffee and our bronze and brass weapons.

I was glad I'd decided not to put on any makeup that morning. Something about apocalyptic times made me not care as much. But I was also a little annoyed I hadn't put on makeup, since we were going for a showdown with my exes.

When we finally entered the cave, we heard the howl again. I wanted to ask if Eve thought it was controlled by Harold or not, but we were too close to the pool.

As we turned the corner, they had definitely been expecting us. In the burbling pool of green goo, individually tied with thick chains, were the three agents, Johnson, Johnson, and Price. Goo dripped from the ceiling and seemed to continuously be coating them.

Posed dramatically were Richard and Veronica with Harold just behind them. He was standing on a rock to make himself seem taller. The rest of the senior dancers and some other classmates were there as well.

"It always takes you so long to come," Richard said.

I let out a very unladylike guffaw that my mom would be proud of, and replied, "Sexual innuendo as an insult? I thought you were more mature than that, Harold. Yeah, I know you're controlling them."

Richard scowled and said, "How did you know?"

"Richard defaults to three insults which boil down saying you're part of the LGBT community, mentally disabled, or enjoy sex too much. Even with this limited reparté, he'd know I would just clap back. By the way, my reply would be, 'That's because of your lack of skill'."

Eve laughed and the blank faced goo-people just continued to stare and pose.

"I knew you'd try to save these people," Harold said through his own lips this time.

I glanced over again at the agents and noticed they were all gagged. Eve had disappeared, but I hoped she was making her way toward them. With a mocking laugh, I replied, "Let me guess, they're immune to the One and your ego was too frail to have them mocking you?" He growled in frustration. This was obviously not going where he wanted. "What was the endgame here with your little action figures all set up to be intimidating? Are you that frail?"

I tried to follow Eve from the corner of my eyes, but I didn't want to be too obvious. She needed more time to unchain the agents.

"I was hoping you'd be impressed, but mostly I was stalling for time until I gained full control of the Hunter."

That was bad, but we knew we'd need to deal with the Hunter one way or another if we wanted to survive until morning. We even made a plan about it. The plan was Eve's unwavering faith in the Agents Johnson.

"How's that going? About as well as you flirting?"

"I almost have it," he said, then cocked his head and asked, "What's wrong with my flirting?" That's what I'd hoped for. He was vain.

"Well, it was pretty weak. The whole 'older man treats you with respect while looking at you like you're a piece of meat' thing is both cliché and kinda ick." I added my best mean girl laugh at the end. It's always nice to insult someone with the truth; it hurts more. He looked like he was about to argue, and I lifted my hand cutting him off, "Before you say the whole 'join me and we can rule the world together' spiel, ew and no."

He turned so red I could see it through the green aura. He sputtered a little then smiled, "Thank you for doing what all little girls like to do and chattering away. I now have control of the Hunter and it's on its way."

"She was stalling too, you budget-priced buffoon." Agent Price almost cackled as she said it. Her hands glowed for a moment before a sword of pure ice appeared in it. Her purple aura blazed. She seemed to have dropped the illusion that made her ridiculously pretty, but kept the elongated canines.

The two Johnsons stood next to her. He had some sort of long pole-axe made of swirling shadow, and she had somehow found her gun. Their yellow and forest green auras also seemed to be shining extra brightly. They must have some sort of magical protection.

The three of them were like action heroes out of an old comic book. I did the only sensible thing and moved away from them.

"The people are innocents. Don't hurt them. Keep your enthusiasm for Harold."

They moved forward and Harold started to laugh, not an evil villain laugh but an unhinged giggle.

Richard and Veronica moved toward the trio and did the most disgusting thing possible. They vomited green goo. It was like watching a firehose set to a wide mist. The mist covered all three of them and their auras became muted. The magical weapons disappeared, and

Agent Kennedy slipped and fell onto her back, the gun going flying into the pool of goo.

Agent Jason reached out and helped Kennedy up. "We're both trained in multiple forms of combat. Can you keep up, Agent Price?"

"I trained in magic and combat at the citadel of New Albion and I have claws." Agent Price's hands didn't turn into claws, but I'm fairly certain she was being metaphorical.

I watched the three of them as they braced to fight with my ex and his sister, and I understood then that the goo had somehow dampened their powers. No wonder it was able to capture them but not take over their minds.

I caught Eve's eye from across the cave and nodded. They might seem like superheroes, but they were no match for the goo-people without powers. I was feeling confident as I sneaked around the cave, until more people came out from the other entrance.

The first was Sergeant Bannerman holding his revolver. My heart raced and I started to sweat. That day on the highway came back to me in a rush, and I just wanted to run.

I swayed in place, paralyzed by panic, waiting for him to turn the gun toward me, but he didn't see me, he saw Eve. He pointed the gun at her and anger overwhelmed my fear. I ran toward him and hit him in the arms with my brass bedpost. The gun went flying. His arms sizzled where I'd hit him, and I followed it up with a swing at his stomach. His stomach seemed to go concave. He stood up and ran out of the cave.

Eve picked up the gun, and I saw her lifting it to aim at Harold. I shook my head, but she didn't see me. Right when I thought she was going to shoot him, she tossed the gun into the pool.

Facing a hoard of raging goo monsters didn't scare me, but a cop with a gun was too real. I'd need to unpack that in therapy.

The mob ran into the cave and all I could do was swing and try to get closer to Harold. If I could just reach him, I could end this. He'd lost control when I threw coffee at him, if I hit him with my bedpost, it might break his connection completely.

Fighting was easy, like a good workout. I could feel them as they attacked and reacted with the reflexes of a lifetime of dance and acrobatics. I felt alive, like I was hitting every mark in a complex choreography that I'd spent my life practising.

When I was finally in front of Harold, I felt like I could end it. I just needed a clear swing.

As I walked toward him, he asked, "Are you going to say it or am I?"

"It's not too late to stop this. You can do better," I said and then in my hammiest voice, I added, "There must be some good in you left."

He said, in a disappointed tone, "I expected you to say 'this ends here', not try some goody-goody speech. But it's not too late to join me."

"Do you offer cookies?" I said and swung for his head. He ducked and was obviously confused. I guess he didn't spend much time online.

I kept trying to hit him, but he was faster than humanly possible and I wasn't very good with the bedpost. Unlike the others, I couldn't sense what he was going to do. Maybe it was because he was giving the orders for the others, or maybe because he wasn't part of the One.

"You're using something to control the One, aren't you? You didn't fully meld with it."

He smiled at me and said, "You're smarter than you look."

"But if this stops magic, how did you do it?" When he hesitated to answer, I swung at him again. He moved out of the way easily.

He glared at me and asked, "How did you know it stops magic?" I gave him a withering glare and tried to poke him with the bedpost. I was getting tired. "I used some of it in the spell. Sort of sympathetic magic."

"I have no idea what that means, but I…" I trailed off. Something was bothering me, my heart was racing, and I felt like dramatic music should be playing. He moved behind me, and I swung in a chopping motion toward him.

He caught the bedpost in one hand and jerked me forward. His hand was smoking and I could hear a sizzling sound. Leaning really close to my face he said, "I'm sorry that something so pretty has to die."

Several things went through my mind just then. My libido hadn't gotten the message that he was the bad guy, my nerves were on edge, my nose swore it smelled bacon, and a little voice in the back of my head said *run*.

I foolishly held on to the bedpost and the little voice changed from run to move left. I twisted my body just in time for the Hunter, which had crept up behind me, to lunge and try to stab me.

It missed me and embedded a blade-like arm all the way through Harold's chest. He let go of the brass bedpost and just stood there smugly. Everyone stopped fighting and watched him. The Hunter stood frozen with its arm inside him. It wasn't any less frightening up close. Its skin seemed to be made of chitin and slime.

Green goo burbled up out of Harold's mouth, and he managed to say, "I control the One. Did you really think this would stop me?" He pushed the blade out and the skin under his once white t-shirt mended itself, leaving nothing but a green scar.

That's when I made the silliest decision I could think of. I took the bedpost and smashed it as hard as I could into what I assumed was the Hunter's head. Then I did it again and again. It suddenly convulsed and fell to the ground. The hard slimy armour was cracked where I hit it, but the goo coming out wasn't green, it was black. I might have cracked its head but that didn't kill it or knock it out.

The thing's aura changed from green to bright gold like Eve and Jordan's. As the aura changed, It smelled of tar and rot with a hint of sweetness. My stomach lurched, and I did my best not to puke.

Harold's eyes grew wide with fear, and he turned and ran.

Small high-pitched clicks came from the Hunter as it moved gracefully toward me. I found myself moving back. *Has it always been this big?* I wondered.

It lashed out with one of its front arms, and I barely moved out of the way in time. It followed up with the other front arm, and I parried it with my bedpost. It was moving slower than I'd seen it move the night before. Maybe I'd done some brain damage, or maybe it hadn't recovered fully from being part of the One. I suddenly preferred it as a goo monster.

We danced, and not the fun kind I preferred; it trying to kill me and me trying to avoid the giant knife arms. I wondered where Eve and the agents were; I could have used some backup. I could hear fighting and grunting, but I couldn't spare the time to see what was going on.

I had never really been in a real fight before, other than sparring in martial arts, and those were fast and over quickly. This was long, and even though I was still in top shape, I was getting tired.

My arms felt like lead and my vision was blurring. My headache was back, but it felt more insistent. I could swear I could hear a voice saying, "I can help you." I assumed it was Harold and ignored it.

Finally, it grazed my leg. Not enough to hit anything, but enough to make me bleed. At first it didn't hurt, and then it was like I'd been hit with lightning. I was worried that it was poisoned.

Both front arms came down, and I was barely able to block them with the bedpost. I could see the blades cutting into it. I held the post above me and pushed as hard as I could, but I was fighting an alien with blades for arms that was the size of a Toyota. I didn't stand a chance.

I fell to my knees and wished I could tell my mom I loved her.

My arms burned, my knees hurt, the cut on my leg had gone oddly numb, but they all paled in comparison to my head. It felt like someone was compressing my brain.

I could feel the strength in my arms leaving and I took a deep breath trying to think. Maybe I could roll out of the way? Doubtful. I was good, but I was hurt and tired and it was hard to think clearly.

Of course, my mind went to Eve. I was disappointed that I wouldn't get to kiss her again. I felt my arms give out, and I said, "I'm sorry, Eve."

Chapter 16

A wild scream echoed through the cave. At first I thought it was me, but it was Eve.

A flash of bronze crossed my vision, and I saw Eve plunge the sword into the crack in the armour on the Hunter's head. I had done just enough damage to let her stab through the damned thing's brain.

Its golden aura flickered and as it started to fade, it clicked, "More will come. You will never be safe."

Standing up, I bashed it again for good measure, and its aura faded out like a light turning off. "Fuck you!" I yelled.

I swayed for a moment and dropped my bedpost. Eve helped prop me up. She wasn't tall, but she was strong. I felt her alien magic healing me a little and the headache lessened.

"Are you okay?" she asked.

My first instinct was to react sarcastically. *Have I always been a bitch or is it just since this summer?* I wondered to myself. Out loud, I said, "Better, thank you."

My words sounded hollow to me, but Eve gave a small smile and went from holding me up to holding my hand.

With the roar in my ears almost gone, I noticed it had gotten quiet, and I saw that all three agents were knocked out. They'd taken out so many goo zombies that the floor was covered with unconscious bodies. I knew the bodies were unconscious, not dead, because I could still see their green fuzzy auras.

For every enemy they'd taken down, there were two more waiting.

Smug, Harold clapped and said, "How touching. It means nothing. You're all going to die down here." He moved faster than I could process. He grabbed Eve by her jacket and tossed her across the room. I heard a crack as her shoulder hit the wall.

I moved to pick up the post, and he grabbed me by the throat. I clawed at his fingers, but even his pinky was too strong for me.

"You are one of the most infuriating women I have ever met. You think you're so hot and you think everyone owes you fealty for that. If the One wasn't taking so much of my energy to control, I would have killed you with magic. You could have been my bride, but instead I'll make sure you're cleaning every toilet in my empire with your tongue."

I couldn't say anything snarky; he was squeezing my throat too tight and I was doing everything I could just to breathe.

Richard and Veronica moved toward us and stood on either side of Harold. He tossed me to the ground. I might not be big, but he tossed me like a doll. I felt the pain in my back, but it felt distant compared to all the rest.

I saw the sibling's mouths opening and I knew what was coming next. They spewed green goo at me. It was warm, acidic, and just generally gross. I may have had fantasies about the two of them and their bodily fluids, but this was a little too monster-porn for my taste.

I felt the goo cover me and I tried not to breathe, but I hadn't gotten a good breath after being tossed. I didn't last long and soon I was choking on goo. I felt the pain in my head get worse, and I could feel Harold's will trying to control me.

It wasn't like when Sergeant Bannerman had puked on me; that was hot and burning. This was stronger, more like something trying to control my mind.

I felt anger and pressure, but as if at a distance, I could have sworn I felt fear.

Help! a soft voice said inside my head.

I felt my resolve fade, and then Harold's voice screamed in my head, *Just give up already! You can't win!* It wasn't a lot, but it was enough to trigger my contrariness.

I resisted and fought to stand up. Veronica and Richard didn't try to stop me. They just stood there confused and stopped vomiting.

Everything was blurry and I was worried that my eyesight had gotten worse, but I had just lost my glasses somewhere in the pool of goo that was impressively halfway up my calf. I expected it to burn when it hit my cut from the Hunter, but it was still just numb.

Harold howled like a crabby toddler who didn't get their way. He sounded so pathetic, I couldn't help but laugh. At least, I tried to laugh; mostly, I burbled and coughed up green goo.

Help! Was that me? Who was asking for help?

I had never been this uncaffeinated or this close to the goo. I could feel Harold still trying to force his will on mine. It was a constant pressure.

He moved toward me, doing the same vampire super-speed schtick. I tried to bat his hand away as he reached for my throat, and I might as well have been hitting a steel wall with a wet spaghetti noodle.

"Let's end this." His breath was warm on my face. The clown needed to start being consistent. He was constantly oscillating between killing and controlling me. I wanted to tell him so, but again I couldn't breathe. Even if I could, I doubt I could have spoken with the amount of goo in my throat and the swelling from his previous choking.

The pressure on my throat started to match the one in my head, and I could feel myself losing consciousness. I couldn't let Harold get the last quip. "One less problem to worry about," I blurted.

Statements he'd made and feelings I'd been having started to coalesce into a picture. The One was fighting him; he wasn't completely in control. He seemed to have a hard time getting it to kill people. Why else would the agents be alive?

Help! the One's voice said more forcefully, and it was definitely the One's voice inside my head.

Is it asking or offering? I wondered.

Both, it replied inside my head. It wasn't words so much as a feeling and images, but I could understand it nonetheless.

Then why have you spent the past week attacking me? I was angry, pained, and the lack of oxygen was making me dizzy.

Its answer was more complicated than before. It felt like everything melted away from me and I was watching a movie. *Is this a flashback?*

I watched miners from a long time ago. The One was in the walls and under the floor of the tunnels. It heard and saw everything, but it didn't understand it. It was curious, like a child.

"They said there was a town here. It's barely a group of houses," said a man in a nice suit.

"We get a share of all the profits; we're going to be rich. The copper is so pure we can practically pick it off the walls," another man, this one in coveralls, replied.

I watched several more scenes with those two in it. Usually the man in the suit was complaining and the second man was overly optimistic.

By the time they found the pool of goo, they were thin, unshaven, and weak from working with little food.

"What's this?" the man in the overalls asked.

"It's gross." The suit wasn't nice anymore, it was stained, ripped, and repaired too many times. "We're going to die down here, you know. And I'm looking forward to it. These bastards conned us into working the mines and we haven't seen a—" he broke off to laugh, "—a cent."

"Come on. Maybe we can just leave?"

"We'll never survive in the woods and make it to civilization. It's too far. I wish I could make those bastards pay." The man sat down on the edge of the pool and, exhausted, promptly fell into it.

Up until then, all I felt from the One was a calm and curious emotion. Once the man entered the pool, his anger and hatred permeated the One. He didn't get controlled by it, he melded with it.

The next visions were bloody and vengeful. The miners became part of the One, joining in on the first man's anger, and they slaughtered everyone. That kind of violence and power was too much for their minds and they started to kill each other. Finally, nature and Northern Ontario winter took the rest.

I was still being choked and everything on me hurt. I had a moment of time to indulge in the pain of me dying before being pulled into another vision.

The One hadn't liked being angry, and it didn't understand why the humans had stopped existing. It didn't understand death or mortality because it couldn't die. It didn't eat like most, it ate magic and the world had plenty of magic to sustain it. It couldn't get bigger or leave the caves, the only reason it could create the pool was because of the mining.

It avoided humans until a new batch started mining. This time, they were better armed and better equipped. The One didn't want to meld with just one human, it wanted to feel and understand more. It started opening up holes and taking the men.

I recognized the story from the diary from the other side. After a month, it had tried to meld with them, but they were all too strong-willed and none were willing. It released one man who was filled with fear and love.

The man returned less than a day later. In his mind the One could see fire. He melded with it and an anger that was strong took the One. The following scenes were the same as before, except that the One felt pain from the gun of the man who escaped to write the diary.

They'd burned his wife at the stake for being a witch, I realized, and I started to cry.

"Crying's not going to save you," sneered Harold.

His face faded away, and I saw a new scene. This time I felt curiosity twice as strong as before as it watched me and Veronica kissing near the pool.

Humans had shown themselves to be finite and dangerous, and the One wanted nothing to do with them, but I smelled like copper and we were doing something it didn't understand.

Richard came in and started to scream, the whole thing played back from the pool's point of view.

When Richard fell in, it felt anger, but it also felt insecurity. Richard melded with it, but he didn't want to murder anyone, he wanted to be like everyone else. Basically, he wanted the same thing every teen wants: to be accepted.

Through Richard, it came to see all the differences there were between people, and despite Richard's need for uniformity, it enjoyed the variety.

It was also fascinated by me; it sensed we were the same. I'm still not sure why, but it wanted to meld with me. Something stopped it every time, and then Harold arrived and used its food to control it. He didn't meld with it, he rode it like a horse, using magic as the reins. It was the equivalent of tying someone up with licorice and forcing them to do what you want.

Okay, maybe licorice is a bad comparison. I did, however, try my best to remember it for later with Eve. If there was a later.

Now it was asking me for help. It wanted to meld with me, and in doing so, try to expel everyone else. It thought that I could be strong enough to fight Harold's control over it.

I was going to die. I knew that. I had the choice of dying or merging with an ancient creature. The first meant I lost my life, the second meant I could lose everything that was me.

You'd think that would give me pause for longer, but I wanted to live and I couldn't let Harold hurt more people.

I'll do it! I shouted in my head.

A calm came over me. The same calm I got when I was really into playing a particular song and it all just flowed. My head stopped hurting for the first time in months. The major emotions I felt from the One were excitement and, once again, curiosity.

I felt the confusion from Richard as he was forcibly expelled from the One and the relief of everyone else.

I opened my eyes and saw Harold. I could perceive far more than just his aura; I could taste his magic. Every magic has a slightly different taste.

The pain in my throat went away as the One and I became, well, one. I guess that's where the name came from.

I gently took Harold's arm and twisted it off my throat. I heard him gasp and saw the bruises I left. I'd have to be more gentle with my new-found strength. We were not going to become killers again, I wouldn't allow it. I might hate the world right now, but that wasn't an excuse to treat it worse than it had treated me.

Eve must have been a better influence than I thought. Had this happened in the summer, I might not have been as certain.

"Shit! Eve," I said and turned away from Harold to go find Eve.

She was lying on the ground where the bastard had thrown her. I could see that her aura was still bright and lovely. I could also see her healing herself. She needed time and energy to heal.

A quick glance around the room showed me that only a few people had been hurt badly enough to stick around. The agents were unconscious and definitely still alive. I was glad no one was too hurt. I could feel the incredible amount of power that the One and I possessed, but it didn't include healing anyone other than myself. Even that was limited; it couldn't really heal me the way Eve could. It could accelerate my own healing, and if I lost parts, it could replace it with goo, but the more that happened the less there would be of me.

"Why aren't you paying attention to me, bitch?" Harold had been ranting and yelling at me while I made sure everyone was okay. It had been surprisingly easy to ignore him. Not having a massive headache was awesome.

"Because you aren't important. You never were. You're just an angry pretty face. I guess we're not that different, except you're a homicidal jackass."

He sputtered incoherently and charged toward me. I sidestepped out of the way at the last second. It was nice to feel strong and graceful again.

I hadn't seen it before, but he was overextending his power. He was spending more of his energy controlling the goo than he could afford. That's why he didn't attack me until I was weakened.

Even now that it wasn't giving him anything but enhanced strength, he still held tight, trying to force his will on the One. My will was stronger and the One *wanted* to listen to me.

I did a pulling motion and ripped the goo from his magical grasp. It flowed out of him like some sort of bad special effect and flew into the pool.

He fell to the ground, panting. Snarling, he said, "Fine. Let's end this."

I rolled my eyes. From somewhere, hopefully some TARDIS magic, he took out a staff. It was made from dark wood and had bright red etching all over it. It glowed with magic for me; no idea if it would for others.

"Nice stick," I said flippantly. But I was already building a defence for Eve and the rest of those that were lying around helpless. Being merged with the One meant I knew what it could do in ways that Harold never could.

"This is the staff of the archmage Alighieri, born from the river Phlegethon. If I activate it, it will destroy everything within a hundred kilometres." He seemed to be trying to smirk and sneer at the same time and ended up just grimacing.

I laughed. "Until this summer, I was a dancer, a popular bitch, and a music nerd." He was obviously confused. "I've read *Dante's Inferno* and know the author's name. I also know you're mixing your Christian and Greek myths. But most of all, I can see magic, and although that staff has lots of fire in it, it will barely fill this room."

He raised the staff and my stomach growled. It was the One and it had expended a lot of energy. We were hungry. I reached out a hand and a gush of goo escaped through it and wrapped around the staff. I pulled it to the same hand and devoured its magic.

Harold swore and screamed, "I still have plenty of magic of my own."

"No," I said. I couldn't help copying his dramatic quick movement from earlier. When I was face to face with him I tapped him on the forehead and cut his connection to magic. It was scarily easy. He crumpled to the ground, and I was alone in a cave with a lot of unconscious people.

"I could use a coffee." I got one of the extra thermoses from my pack and sat down next to Eve to drink a coffee. I couldn't wake anyone, and I figured the danger was over for now.

The coffee was fresh and tasted just as good as before. I wondered why I wasn't being burned the way the other goo-people had. The answer appeared in my head. I had the goo inside me since that summer and even more when I'd been spewed in my eyes. The whole time I fought it, I drank coffee, and over that time, with the help from Eve's healing, the goo inside me became immune to the copper. It would be different if someone stabbed me with the brass sword, but I wouldn't melt, thankfully.

I'd just finished half the thermos when a stream of soldiers with their guns raised came into the cave. I recognized the logo on their uniform from Agent Price's business card. They must be Elmsley, which meant Harold was their problem now.

The woman in charge had long, dark red hair tied in a tight bun. The streak of white hair was more ornamental than indicative of ageing. She had three maple leaves on her uniform that meant she was some sort of General.

I knew she was in charge, because when they came in, she pointed at me and said, "If it moves, shoot it."

Chapter 17

I wanted to say something pithy or scathing, but the woman, whose aura was red, which I was beginning to suspect meant wizard, wouldn't take it. I'm not sure if a hail of bullets would kill me, but it certainly would kill the people laying around.

Gently I put down the coffee and raised my hand.

The general said, "I am Lieutenant-General Lanthier. Who are you?"

"I'm Helen Benson, high school student."

The woman squinted at me. She then put on a pair of pince-nez glasses and squinted at me some more. I could tell they were magical, but what they did, I had no idea.

"Miss Benson, I'm sorry to tell you that you and everyone in this cave have been compromised and will require cleansing." That didn't sound good, so why was she so pleased?

"Wait, are you saying you're going to shoot me?" I asked, panicked.

Giving me a scathing glare, she said, "No, the entire area will be bombed once we take Second-Lieutenant Harnel back for questioning and testing."

Surprised, I replied, "What about Agent Price?"

"She was here unsanctioned and knew the risks." Two men picked up Harold and the whole group marched out of the cave.

I was trying to decide what to do when the agents started waking up. I went over to them and said, "I get that you are probably woozy and tired and all that, but some General woman just came in and said that the area was going to be bombed. Do something."

Agent Price said, "Lanthier" as if it were a swear word.

Jason spun around and said, "Why don't we have any goo on us?"

"I pulled it out. I've merged with the One and it turns out the goo wasn't evil, we humans are. We're safe now, except for the fact that Agent Price's people have taken Harold and are going to bomb us."

Agent Price took a cell phone from somewhere and she called someone. I seriously needed to know how people kept pulling things out of nowhere. She explained what was going on and at the end she said, "Yes, General, I understand." She hung up and swore.

"Give me the phone," Kennedy asked. She dialled the phone and said, "Sir, we have a problem." She paused and listened before responding, "Yes, Elmsley." Another pause. "Bullshit, you know I'm immune to mind effects." There was more conversation, but the One was telling me that it had tried to take over Agents' Johnson and Johnson's mind, but couldn't.

She hung up and told us, "*My* General will try to declare this an *alien* thing and bring it into our jurisdiction. He'll call back."

Without any further talking, we all moved toward helping those that were still unconscious. By the time the General called back, everyone but Eve was awake.

Kennedy put the phone on speaker and the General said, "Because of the presence of the Hunter and the Princess, I was able to convince the Minister of Defence that Elmsley was overstepping. It helped that he didn't want to deal with the fallout of bombing Northern Ontario. Agent Price, I spoke to General Stuart, and you're to coordinate with Kennedy and Jason on this. I'm sending a squad of medics, and I want clean bills of health from the entire town before I lift quarantine."

"Thank you, sir," Kennedy said warmly. It was a funny contrast to the General's terseness.

Eve woke up then and said, "Did we win?"

I helped her up and gently kissed her cheek. "We're alive, so yeah, I think we won."

I poured her some coffee from the thermos and told her everything that happened. When I was done, she sat there bemused. After a long silence, she asked, "So do you bleed green now?" There was no disgust or worry in her voice, just curiosity.

"I don't know. Would you still like me if I did?"

"Of course, but you'd have to be super careful. People freak out about things like that in most places." She looked distracted by memories and then snapped back and stared into my eyes. "They're still grey. How come?"

That I knew was my choice. I closed my eyes and opened them; by her gasp, I could tell they'd turned green. "Can you do any other colours?"

I concentrated on the colour orange as hard as I could and closed my eyes. When I opened them, she smiled and said, "I love Halloween, but that's a little creepy."

As we talked, the medical teams arrived and cleared everyone for normal life quickly. Except for me. I spent almost the entire day being poked and prodded. I gave enough blood that I knew I didn't bleed green. The One didn't need to exert any effort on my physiology because I was both willing and fully melded.

Near dinner, my mom showed up at the cave with food for everyone. "Are you okay?" she asked as she hugged me tightly.

"Yes, I'm fine. Eve ate your cookies in the roasting room," I replied.

"Hey!" Eve protested.

Rolling her eyes, my mom said, "I talked to Fred. It's okay. Probably for the best since those were healing cookies. But I mean it, you melded with something that both alien and magical experts don't understand. Are you okay?"

"Yes, I'm okay. I actually feel better than I have in weeks. Although I'm going to need new glasses. Mine were destroyed in an epic battle." I didn't pause before asking, "Did you bring me coffee?"

My mom put her hands on her hips and said, "Helen Judy Benson, do you think I would force my way past a military blockade, learn that you might be hurt, and then stop to get you coffee?" She paused for a moment and added, "Of course I did."

"Thanks, Mom. You're the best!"

We spent a quiet Halloween in a cave with a bunch of doctors, and in the end it was Agent Kennedy Johnson that came to talk to me. "We've done a whole bunch of tests and as far as our doctors are concerned, you are completely healthy. I checked your blood tests and talked with an expert at Westmeath University. Your blood has white, red, and bio-metallic green cells. The new cells seem to work as a combination repair and backup for your white cells, but they do not survive long after being outside of your body. We also saw a decline in the health of the red and white cells afterward."

"What does that mean?" my mom asked.

"It means that as far as I can tell your daughter is completely healthy, but it's our opinion that if she separates from the One, she'll have only a few months to live. As long as they stay together, however, she will live a very long life."

Eve grabbed my arm in a hug and said, "Good, 'cause I'm keeping her."

EPILOGUE

After that day, everything turned around. The town treated me like a hero. I joined dance again, and everyone loved me. They even built a statue in my honour.

They totally didn't.

I was still treated like a murderer and the town didn't take me and Eve being a couple very well. Fuck them.

Despite me being nearly indestructible and having a girlfriend that can heal, I still get heart palpitations when I see a cop. I haven't been able to meet Sergeant Bannerman's eyes since. If I'm being honest, I still flinch when someone gets too close to me, and I still worry about the town taking action.

One thing that amazed me was how fast the people of Ansonville got over the entire town being mind controlled. Dean had his party two days late, and after that, he was the only one willing to talk about what happened. He was still a sleaze, but it felt more and more like an act.

Richard settled on spending the next few months pretending I wasn't there and then just glaring at me. I heard he's going to a school in the States on a hockey scholarship.

The biggest surprise for me was Veronica. She quit dance and completely changed her aesthetic and attitude, becoming a knock-off punk rocker. She started a new band, ironically called D-Nigh. They're not bad, although a little screechy for my taste.

Fred kept bringing presents and now I have enough equipment to stock a small restaurant.

We survived the semester and then the next.

Eve continued to join me bi-weekly in Timmins for martial arts classes, and she convinced me to join band class. It was fun, but mostly I liked making music with her on our own. Get your mind out of the gutter! Yeah, we did that too, but I was actually talking about real music.

I was accepted at the University of Ottawa, Westmeath University, and Baker University, mostly thanks to an amazing reference letter from Doctor Batudev, who turned out to be Agent Kennedy Johnson's brother.

Today, Eve and I packed up my little mini and are heading to Baker. She can't go back to Westmeath because there's too much alien activity, and from everything Bart told me, Baker is a great place for two people who are weird and don't want to stand out.

Speaking of Bart, he's even gotten us rooms in a house near campus. We're supposed to check it out with him and his girlfriend Francine when we arrive. Just in case that falls through, my mom can get us rooms over the Dancing Goat franchise there.

I'm going to miss my mom, but university awaits. It's a big adventure, but after the year I've had, I'm sure it'll be a walk in the park.

"You ready to go?" Eve asked.

"Hell yes!" I am *so* ready to leave this town.

Character Appearances

Many of the characters in this book have been woven into the Aetherverse. If you'd like to read more about them, here are the books you can find them in.

Helen and Cheryl Benson

Mentioned or short appearances in *The Gates of Westmeath* series by Jen and Éric Desmarais. *Assassins! Accidental Matchmakers, Monsters! Incidental Wedding Guests*, and *Fanatics! Inevitable Honeymoon Crashers* (expected in 2026).

Evanna "Eve" Swan

Secondary character in *The Gates of Westmeath* series by Jen and Éric Desmarais. *Assassins! Accidental Matchmakers*, and *Monsters! Incidental Wedding Guests*.

Minor character in the *Lucky in Love* series by Jen Desmarais. *Crushing It* and *Winging It*.

Doctor Tommy Batudev (Née Fairfield)

Secondary character in *The Gates of Westmeath* series by Jen and Éric Desmarais. *Assassins! Accidental Matchmakers, Monsters! Incidental Wedding Guests, Fanatics! Inevitable Honeymoon Crashers* (expected in 2026), and *Connections! The Unexpected First Collection* (November 2025).

Main character of the *Lucky in Love* series by Jen Desmarais. *Crushing It* and *Winging It*. Appears in The Siren's Song Volume 3 in the short story *Snow Day*.

Jordan the Arinitian

Secondary character in *The Mystery of the Dancing* Lights by Éric Desmarais.

Bart "Brick" Mortar

Secondary character in *The Baker City Mysteries* by Éric Desmarais. *A Study in Aether, The Sign of Faust, A Case of Synchronicity*, and *The Mystery of the Dancing Lights*.

Katherine "Kitty" Price

Main character of *Parasomnia* by Éric Desmarais.

Small appearances in *Everdome* and *Mystery of the Dancing Lights* by Éric Desmarais.

Kennedy and Jason Johnson

Main characters of *The Gates of Westmeath* series by Jen and Éric Desmarais. *Assassins! Accidental Matchmakers, Monsters! Incidental Wedding Guests, Fanatics! Inevitable Honeymoon Crashers* (expected in 2026), and *Connections! The Unexpected First Collection* (November 2025).

Mentioned briefly in *The Mystery of the Dancing Lights* by Éric Desmarais.

Lieutenant-General Lanthier

Appears in *The Mystery of the Dancing Lights* by Éric Desmarais.

General Stuart

Appears in *Parasomnia, A Case of Synchronicity*, and *The Mystery of the Dancing Lights*, by Éric Desmarais. Also *Monsters! Incidental Wedding Guests* by Jen and Éric Desmarais.

Acknowledgements

Some books take longer than others and some need the right inspiration. I could have never finished this book without my wonderful wife and co-author Jen Desmarais. She inspires me constantly. Without her, this book would be extremely different.

I would like to acknowledge that this book was written on the unceded, unsurrendered Territory of the Anishinaabe Algonquin Nation, and pay my respects to elders both past and present.

I'd also like to thank my weekly tabletop role playing groups for helping me test out monsters and settings. You guys make all the work worth it.

To the team at River City Siren Press, thank you for your enthusiasm and all the hard work you put into this book.

Last but not least, this book wouldn't exist without both my kids. I wrote the first part with a month old Keladry wiggling on my lap and the second with a giggling two year old Adrien in the background. Thank you for your love, patience, and for showing me a different way of looking at the world.

About the Author

Éric has had an eclectic career which ranges from casino dealer to canal boat captain to radio station DJ. He has worked for the federal government since 2007 in various roles including media monitoring, web development, typesetting, layout, desktop publishing, and web and document accessibility. During his off time, he works as a freelance typesetter for multiple authors and publishers, roasts gourmet flavoured coffee, runs several pen-and-paper role-playing games, writes, and helps run JenEric-Designs.ca (home of the TravellingTARDIS.com). His blog, JenEric Movie Reviews, was nominated for an Aurora Award in 2023.

He lives in Ottawa, Ontario with his wife, daughter, and son. Visit him at www.EricDesmarais.ca.

Other Works by Éric Desmarais

The Gates of Westmeath

1. Assassins! Accidental Matchmakers
1.5 Connections! The Unexpected First Collection (November 2025)
2. Monsters! Incidental Wedding Guests
3. Fanatics! Inevitable Honeymoon Crashers (2026)

Baker City Mysteries
(Elizabeth Investigates)

1. A Study in Aether
2. The Sign of Faust
3. A Case of Synchronicity
3.5 Coffee Shop Between the 'Verses
4. The Mystery of the Dancing Lights

Other Aetherverse Books

Everdome
Parasomnia

About River City

River City Siren Press is a small press publisher based out of the Richmond, Virginia area. RCSP primarily publishes fantasy, science fiction, and poetry, but we dabble in most genres. Our authors are from all over the world and represent people from all walks of life and diverse life experiences. We are passionate about marginalized voices, stories, and characters. Email us at rivercitysirenpress@gmail.com or check out our website at www.rivercitysirenpress.com to learn more about our authors, books, and literary magazine, The Siren's Song.

The Baker City Mysteries

A Study in Aether

Elizabeth Coderre has always known that there was something strange about her home town, Baker Ontario, but it isn't until her English teacher disappears that she starts to find out how strange. Getting through classes, killer kitten swarms, and bullies are going to be the easy parts of surviving at Sir Arthur Conan Doyle High. Elizabeth and her best friends, Jackie and Angela, are up to the challenge... they hope.

The Sign of Faust

Elizabeth Coderre solves mysteries. Magic, wizards, and killer kittens didn't stop her last semester. Now someone is trying to kill her in absurdly complicated ways, she's hearing voices, her best friends are constantly fighting despite being madly in love, and the desires of Baker City's residents are becoming reality. Can she find out who's trying to kill her and discover the source of everyone's luck, while navigating dating, concerts, school, and competing in the science Olympics? She can only wish... and you know what they say about wishes!

A Case of Synchronicity

Elizabeth Coderre loves mysteries. She's faced down deranged Hags, killer kittens, wiley Artificers, and evil Genies, all with the help of her two best friends. Now she's stuck in summer 1985, Jackie is in a coma, and Angela is quarantined. Can Elizabeth cope with her inner demons, the 80's, and a new voice in her head? Can Angela save Jackie and the entire Bytown Memorial Hospital? This is going to be the least relaxing March break, but can they solve the mystery... in time?

The Mystery of the Dancing Lights

Mysteries are Elizabeth Coderre's life, and after wizards, hags, artificers, vampires, kobolds, genies, and killer kittens, she thinks she's seen everything. She's wrong! And when she goes to Riding Thorpe summer camp, which is built on an old government experimental facility, she discovers that there's a lot she doesn't know.

Can she solve the mystery of the dancing lights, save her friends, and escape a time loop? Or is she cursed to relive her friends' deaths forever?

The Gates of Westmeath

Assassins! Accidental Matchmakers

Kennedy Fairfield just graduated in the class of 2002, and is now trying to find her purpose in life, or at least a job in her field. When she saves Jason Johnson, the leader of a secret Community of supernatural people called Aetherborn, from an attempted assassination, they embark on a whirlwind epic romance and adventure.

For Kennedy and Jason to discover why people are disappearing in time to save her friends, they'll have to face teleporting assassins, grumpy wizards, gossiping hags, mafia robots, and secret military groups, all in the city of Westmeath, Ontario, which has more secrets than residents.

Monsters! Incidental Wedding Guests

The week before Kennedy and Jason's wedding is busy. There are cake tastings, dress fittings, a formal ball, and, as their superhero personas the Phantom and the Wraith, fighting monsters.

These behemoths are destructive, smell like snack food, and are only after one thing: Door Tech Industries technology.

Adding to the chaos are their friends and families; Jason's grandmother has returned after having been missing for half a century, Kennedy's mom is dead-set on keeping things traditional, and Jason's best friend is kidnapped before the rehearsal.

Kennedy and Jason just want to get married, preferably before the next monster attack.

LUCKY IN LOVE

CRUSHING IT

After an epic grounding for some bad decisions with even worse friends, Tommy is lucky to even go to the Door Tech March Break camp. There, he crosses paths with Carter Batudev, and chemistry isn't just for the classroom. With love and a renewed interest in STEM, Tommy returns home to Parry Sound, where, to the relief of his parents, he makes better friends, and joins the STEM club.

When the club goes to the province-wide competition in Toronto, he's reunited with Carter, whose team is also competing. Thus ensues a wild long weekend full of romance, hijinks, STEM, and singing.

This book takes place in an alternate world where technology is more advanced, especially in Westmeath, due to in-universe reasons.

WINGING IT

A wedding and a summer camp that Tommy and Carter are never going to forget.

Tommy discovers magic exists, his boyfriend is a rock giant, and his sister is marrying one of the leaders of a supernatural community called Aetherborn.

Carter learns to navigate an in-person relationship, introducing Tommy to the magical world, and being involved in his Ariki's wedding.

Both boys need to build their confidence in each other, themselves, and their relationship. The Door Tech summer camp seems to be the perfect way to do that, until they get magically transported to the not-so-fictional world of Everdome. In this realm of Domed continents floating in space, winged beasts, and new cultures, the boys will have to overcome challenges beyond anything they've seen before.

The only way they, and their relationship, can survive is if they start Winging It!

PARASOMNIA

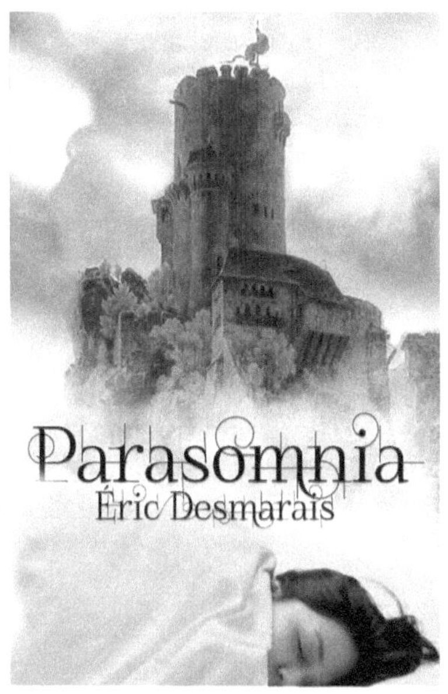

At the Aux-Anges institute, nestled in the woods outside of North Bay, they study and treat parasomnias, or sleep disorders.

Ashley suffers from night terrors, Terrance sleepwalks, Kiri sleep-eats, and Paul sets fires; they are there for treatment. Adelaide took the job as a counselor to discover why she still has an imaginary friend.

When they discover the secret hideout of an old club called the Dreamers, they are shocked to find that the five of them are connected through more than just the Institute.

THE LOST HEIR(S)

The Imaginarium is the magical world where stories are given life. Existing behind every mirror. It is a reflection of what we believe. It is the realm where heroes live. Hercules, Achilles, Robin Hood, Zorro.

Albert Drake doesn't come close to qualifying.

He never wanted to be a hero but that's exactly what The Imaginarium needs from him. Now Albert, his twin sister Becca, and his best friend have to team up with creatures they've only ever killed in video games to stop a boss-tier Dark Lord from a magical realm intent on killing them to stop a prophecy they've never heard of.

GEORGIE KARRAS AND THE NIDDLE OF NERN

Nothing has been right since Georgie's father died in the war. Her friendships fell apart. She fell apart. And then one night, she follows a familiar green light into a world fighting its own darkness. In the Kingdom of Nern, Georgie will uncover family secrets and race to stop a growing darkness that is devouring all the color and good in a kingdom more vibrant and wonderful than she ever imagined possible.

FORTITUDE

This is a world of Giants, Titans, corrupt gods, and shattered empires. Desperate to avoid extinction, the Jattarian war machine grinds on, fueled by the blood of children. Thyra and Agnor will have to find the Virtues within as their paths take them in opposite directions as they grow in Fortitude to save themselves and those closest to them. This is a dual point-of-view military fantasy that explores the coming of age stories of two teens battling for honor and survival. Join Thyra and Agnor on an epic journey to find Fortitude.